D1220380

THE BERMUDA SHIPWRECK

ERIC MURPHY

Copyright © 2016 Eric Murphy
This edition copyright © 2016 Dancing Cat Books,
an imprint of Cormorant Books Inc.
First published in the United States of America in 2017.

No part of this publication may be reproduced, stored in a retrieval system or transmitted,
in any form or by any means, without the prior written consent of the publisher or a
licence from The Canadian Copyright Licensing Agency (Access Copyright). For an Access
Copyright licence, visit www.accesscopyright.ca or call toll free 1.800.893.5777.

 Canada Council **Conseil des Arts** **for the Arts** **du Canada**

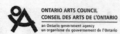

Canadian Patrimoine
Heritage canadien **Canada**

The publisher gratefully acknowledges the support of the Canada Council for the Arts
and the Ontario Arts Council for its publishing program. We acknowledge
the financial support of the Government of Canada through the Canada Book Fund (CBF)
for our publishing activities, and the Government of Ontario through the Ontario
Media Development Corporation, an agency of the Ontario Ministry of Culture,
and the Ontario Book Publishing Tax Credit Program.

LIBRARY AND ARCHIVES CANADA CATALOGUING IN PUBLICATION

Murphy, Eric, 1952–, author
The Bermuda shipwreck / Eric Murphy.

Issued in print and electronic formats.
ISBN 978-1-77086-479-5 (paperback). — ISBN 978-1-77086-484-9 (html)

I. Title.

PS8626.U754B47 2016   JC813'.6   C2016-904408-4
C2016-904409-2

United States Library of Congress Control Number: 2016945344

Cover design: angeljohnguerra.com
Interior text design: Tannice Goddard, bookstopress.com

Printed and bound in Canada.
Manufactured by Friesens in Altona, Manitoba, Canada in October, 2016.

This book is printed on 100% post-consumer waste recycled paper.

DANCING CAT BOOKS
An imprint of Cormorant Books Inc.
10 ST. MARY STREET, SUITE 615, TORONTO, ONTARIO, M4Y 1P9
www.dancingcatbooks.com
www.cormorantbooks.com

Chapter One

Paradise Lost

*Motorsailer: A boat that relies equally on motor and sail
for propulsion, often over long distances.*

*Will couldn't tell if the person sitting in the open boat was alive or
dead. Will treaded water as he stared at the face covered in gauze,
sunglasses, and a floppy hat tied under their chin. To Will's right was
an equally strange sight. A man in a black suit appeared to be sitting
on the water, his dark skin contrasting with his long blond curls. He
pulled a wedge of orange from a basket and held it out for Will. His
sad expression grew concerned as he looked to the figure in the boat
who sat still as death. The hands didn't tell Will if it was a man or
a woman because they were covered in gauze gloves. Suddenly, the
gauzed left hand rose toward Will, who jerked back in surprise. The
covered hand held out four old-fashioned envelopes, letting the first
three blank ones fall away till only the last one, which had "H.M.S.
Lily" written on it, remained. Just as the ink on the envelope started
to run, as if it was wet, the person's right hand pointed a gun at Will
and fired.*

Bang! The sound pulled Will from his dream. His cousin, Harley,
reacted to the explosive sound by throwing the helm over hard.

The change in course hurled Will from *Wavelength*'s banquette where he had been sleeping. He whipped his arms up defensively as he sailed out of the cockpit and plowed into the warm Bermuda water. Now fully awake, he whipped the salt water from his face with a double headshake. The life ring Harley threw at him scythed through the air and splashed within reach behind him.

"Will! Are you all right?" she screamed, her face scrunched with concern.

Will arced his right arm over and touched his head in the scuba divers' signal that said he was okay. Harley's look of concern told him she hadn't done it as a joke. He also knew that, for a seventeen-year-old, she was both serious and safety-conscious when it came to boating.

To show her he really was okay, he ignored the life ring and got back to the motorsailer with a few strokes of Australian crawl. Harley flipped the ladder over the stern and he clambered aboard, then hauled the life ring back in.

"What happened?" he asked, wiping his face and hands with the towel she handed him.

"Don't know. I heard the crack and I turned her into the wind in case it was the rigging. Never imagined you'd be thrown clear. But I think it came from below deck. Here, take the wheel and I'll have a look."

She started up the diesel and slipped it into gear, giving it just enough throttle to stop the wind from pushing them off course. The shoals and reefs in Bermuda had claimed ships for centuries. It wouldn't do to let your ship drift off course when your depth gauge fluctuated between thirty and twelve feet.

Harley spun around and skipped down the companionway backward. She lifted the floorboard grate on the starboard side to stare at the water tank. That one hadn't worked since before they'd sailed from Nova Scotia. The owner, a Mr. Bennett, had told Harley that it leaked but that he was sure the port-side water tank would be all two people would need for the short sail to Bermuda, especially as they could refill it as they moored in ports along the way to their final destination.

Harley's face was scrunched in surprise as she ran a finger along the edge of the tank before lifting the top, which hinged backward.

"Somebody cut it open and put a hinge on it," she said, staring inside.

The light from the portholes showed a piece of equipment the size of a small ottoman sitting on the bottom of the tank. She held up the frayed end of a red ratchet strap.

"This wore through till it snapped from the tension exerted on it by this, whatever this is," she said, peering at it more closely.

"Well what is it?" asked Will.

"Some kind of pump, and there are coils of hose here too." She shook her head before adding, "Weird. Why did Bennett tell us the tank had a leak?"

"Maybe it had a leak so he used it to store stuff," offered Will.

"No. Tanks are supposed to be sealed. Somebody deliberately cut into this tank. There's something fishy about this."

Harley scampered back topside and dropped the sails in order to motor the remaining distance. Harley called Bennett with the cell he'd given her, to say that they were close to the rendezvous point and to inform him about the broken strap in the water tank. A man called Drury answered and said Bennett was out but that he'd relay the message.

An hour later, they dropped anchor about a mile off shore. Their gear was packed and ready to leave when Drury roared across the water in his sixteen-foot Zodiac, which was rigged like a dive boat. After tying up in the lee of the motorsailer, he introduced himself as a friend of the owner's.

"That's nice gear you have there," said Will, nodding to the new-looking wetsuits and dive gear in the Zodiac.

"You dive?" asked Drury.

Will grinned. "I got my license three days before we set sail from Nova Scotia so we could dive while we're here."

"So what is that gear we found in the water tank?" asked Harley.

Harley's tone was neutral but the question made Drury look away.

"It's some kind of pump, isn't it?" she pressed.

"It's a backup bilge pump," said Drury.

"What? No it's not. Way too big. It's a pump and with all those lengths of hose, it's for a lot more than a bilge," said Will smiling, thinking Drury was kidding.

"Well, I'm not much of a boat guy, I just assumed it was," said Drury, not looking them in the eye. He asked if they'd reported the hoses to the customs officials when they had stopped in at St. George to sign the papers.

"We just found them so we couldn't have reported them. But why are you concerned about what we reported to customs. Is this some kind of contraband?" asked Harley, her eyes narrowing.

Drury pulled a pistol from his backpack, and pointed it at the cousins. "It's too bad you found that equipment, because now it changes everything."

Chapter Two

Dive or Die

*BCD: A buoyancy-compensating device in the shape of a vest,
secured to an air tank and which can be inflated or deflated
to give scuba divers neutral buoyancy.*

Drury locked them in the front cabin where Will had slept. After
motoring for an hour, he dropped anchor. They heard a splash.
For twenty minutes, the quiet was only disturbed by the wind in
the rigging, and then they heard him climb aboard. He opened the
cabin door, pointed to the water tank with his gun, and ordered
them to carry the pump and the hoses to the cockpit. Then they
secured a screen off of *Wavelength*'s stern.

His diving gear was wet and he pointed to an inflated marker
that bobbed at the surface about thirty yards from where they had
anchored.

"You're right, it's not a bilge pump. It's an underwater vacuum
and you're going to use it on the wreck that's at the end of that
diving marker. That screen we've just set up will allow me to see
what's been sucked up from the ocean floor. You're looking to find
an opening in the hull so you can get in and bring up a wooden
box that sank with her. Box's about two feet by two feet. The
initials *P.B.* are carved on the front. Got that? *P.B.*? Two tugs on

the line and I start the pump. Two more and I stop. You get me the box and I'll let you go. Got that?"

"What's the wreck? And what's in the box?" asked Will.

"You don't need to know that. The less you know, the better," said Drury.

Harley shook her head. "Will's had no diving experience beyond his certification so there's no way he's ready for wreck diving. I'll go down alone and check it out."

"Best if you alternate using the vacuum so you don't get tired. And I bet that box will need two people to pull it free," said Drury. "Besides," he added with a crooked smile, "it's not safe to dive without a buddy."

"It's not safe for a thirteen-year-old novice diver to go into a wreck. I'm not going to let this happen," said Harley, crossing her arms.

"It's dive or die," said Drury, swinging his pistol from Will to Harley.

The warm Bermuda breeze tugged at the checkered shirt's rolled-up sleeve as if trying to entice Drury to put down his weapon.

Drury tossed an empty juice bottle over the side, raised his automatic, and pointed it at the quart-sized container. Pulled along by an incoming tide, it bobbed twenty feet from their sail-boat. He squeezed off two shots that kicked up a little spray on either side of the bottle — close enough. Arguing with Drury was more dangerous than wreck diving.

The ejected bullet casings clattered into the cockpit.

"Hey," yelped Will as one of the hot casings ricocheted and singed his bare foot. Drury grinned as he retrieved the shells.

Will and Harley zipped up their wetsuit jackets and the zippers that ran up their calves, making it easier to get into and out of the black neoprene. Harley clambered down the ladder to the Zodiac Drury had tethered in the lee of the sixty-foot motorsailer.

Drury helped Will with his gear. He retrieved air tanks from the plywood tank holder strapped to the steering console. Although just seventeen, Harley had been diving since she was Will's age, which explained why she was so at ease with all the gear.

As Will wiggled into his buoyancy compensator, Harley draped his regulator hose over his chest, and tucked the emergency regulator into the pocket of his BCD — his "buoyancy-compensating device." She opened the valves on both their air tanks, which hissed as the pressure was released to the mouthpiece on their regulators. With his weight belt secured, Will sat on the Zodiac's rubber bumper.

Harley dipped their fins into the ocean — wet fins were easier to pull on. Will winced as he slipped his over the little red dot the hot bullet casing had left on the top of his left foot.

They sprayed and rubbed anti-fog liquid into their masks, rinsed, then snugged them on. They clamped their regulators between their teeth and took a breath. Harley picked up the net bag and on her nod, they held on to their masks with their right hands, then toppled backwards into the ocean warmed by the bright island sun. To anybody on the distant shore, they looked like tourists on a leisurely dive.

When they popped their heads above the surface, Will gave his inflator tube two blasts. That swelled the BCD's air bladder so he could float effortlessly, and he switched to his snorkel to save air. Harley reached over and double-checked the air pressure on his gauge — just below three thousand pounds per square inch, or psi. Harley was adamant that every dive end at seven hundred psi so that they would reach the Zodiac with five hundred psi in reserve. This three-in-one gauge also told you how deep you were, while the compass helped you navigate in deep water or in an enclosed space like a cave or a wreck.

Drury stood on the deck with his hands on his hips as they

swam out to the big, red flotation ball that held their dive line in place. With her back to Drury, Harley pulled the snorkel from her mouth and said, "So let's see if we can find that box to keep our jailer happy and maybe find out what this is really about, okay?" Her tone was upbeat but Will knew she was grinning to keep his morale up.

They put their index fingers to their thumbs to create an "O," the divers' sign that everything was okay. They thumbed the button that let the air out of their BCDs, then sank beneath the swells. A red hind, about two feet in length, swam up to investigate, hovering at mask height.

The blurbing sound of escaping bubbles accompanied them down to where the dive rope was tied to a coral-encrusted iron railing on the wreck that rested on the ocean floor. They also heard the muffled sound of gunshots. The bullets fizzed harmlessly away as Drury continued his target shooting.

Will's flippers released a small cloud of dust as they touched the bottom. He tilted his head back, pressed the top of his mask against his forehead and exhaled through his nose to rid his mask of water that had seeped in. That small act of controlling his environment calmed him.

Moments after they tugged on the rope, they heard the compressor vibrating as it vacuumed the ocean floor and brought its contents up to Drury. The sediment released through the screen was carried by the current, well past *Wavelength*'s stern, where it fell back to the ocean floor, spreading out in a cone shape too murky to see through.

Will marveled at how clear the water in front of him was in the bright, midday sun as they took turns holding the two handles on the vacuum. Harley was handling the hose on her own when she suddenly exposed a rusted steel hull about eight inches below the sand.

Harley looked up long enough to point a finger at him then at the hose to indicate she'd like him to take over.

He took over the vacuum hose and pointed it at the front end of the trough Harley had created along the periphery of whatever boat was lying here. The decades of sand that had been piled up over the steel structure from current, tide and storms suddenly gave way to an opening. It was a gash in the metal. Will gave the cord a double tug so Drury turned off the compressor, whose humming died away.

Will and Harley peered into the hull's gaping wound. She pulled their underwater writing tablets out of the net bag so they could use them to fan the sand away in a gentler manner than the vacuum could. A moment later, she held her left hand up for him to stop, reached into the sand, and pulled up a small, encrusted, rectangular box that looked big enough to hold reading glasses. When she tried to open it, the box broke and they saw it held a gold necklace with a thumbnail-sized emerald pendant that was framed by what looked to be golden lobster claws. Harley's eyes were wide with delight as she showed it to him.

They tucked the necklace into the net bag, gave the rope two tugs and resumed vacuuming the sand from the four-foot-wide furrow that ran quite a length along the steel hull. The coral reef had probably sliced into the boat, causing it to sink, thought Will as he turned the vibrating vacuum hose head to the task at hand.

A moment later, they bumped into a steel box which they wrestled out of the opening, careful not to rub up against the steel edges that might inflict a nasty cut. Time and rust had welded the box shut tight. It resisted their attempts to pry it open. When they turned back to the opening they froze. Inches from where the box had lain, was a skeleton's hand reaching out to them.

Chapter Three

A Watery Grave

Bimini: An open-front, detachable fabric cover for a boat's cockpit.

Will and Harley stared at the skeleton hand. Had its owner tried to get the box off the boat before it sank? wondered Will, who gave a little shudder at the sight of the bones.

As they vacuumed up more sand, the arms, chest, legs, and skull revealed themselves. They were careful not to suck up pieces of bone.

Will and Harley had to flatten themselves so their tanks didn't snag on the top of the hull's ragged opening. A bit of light showed through a hole about thirty yards past them. It wasn't enough to see by, so they pulled underwater flashlights from the net bag and turned them on. The two beams crossed like spotlights.

When Will hovered over the skeleton he made a little "Oh" that popped the respirator out of his mouth. Harley snagged it and gave it back to him. Will slipped it back in and, to avoid inhaling water, activated the purge valve. His heart had skipped a beat when he'd lost access to air, so he made sure he stayed calm.

Harley questioned him with the "Okay?" sign. He responded by arcing an arm up and touching his head with his fingers for emphasis before pointing out what had startled him.

Harley fluttered closer and saw the hole in the front of the skull. She carefully vacuumed sand on the far side of the skeleton. Something clumped through the hose and banged its way up — possibly the bullet that had pierced the skeleton's skull, thought Will.

As they were fanning the sand with their marker boards, the pump stopped and they felt the tug rope jerk twice. Drury wanted them to come up.

Harley attached a thin, braided line of nylon rope to the box they'd pulled from the wreck. From the net bag she pulled out and unrolled a flotation bag, which she inflated by putting the emergency regulator in it and activating her purge valve button. It wasn't big enough to float the box on its own but it did make it a lot easier to bring it up.

Drury was in the Zodiac when they surfaced by the flotation ball. He saw the inflated bag, smiled excitedly and tossed them a line, which Harley secured to the box before he started hauling it over.

When it was abreast of the Zodiac, Will and Harley kicked their fins and pushed from below while Drury hoisted it from above till they wrestled the box into the bottom of the boat. He took their fins, helped them negotiate the ladder, then helped them shed their BCD's and tanks. They moved the steel box into the sailboat's large cockpit where they sat panting and dripping while Drury dashed below to fetch a crowbar.

He tried to pry the padlock open with the crowbar, but it didn't yield. He slipped the crowbar in place and slammed his foot down on it. The lock snapped open. It still took some prying before the rust weld cracked open to reveal it was empty — except for a single coin and a bullet that had no cartridge attached to it.

It was hard to say who was most disappointed. After a moment, Will rolled the bullet in his hand and asked, "Why did you signal for us to come up?"

Drury reached for a tray sitting on the pilothouse top and retrieved two round discs tarnished from their time in the sea.

"These came up through the vacuum. They're the same as this coin from the box. You see any more of these down there?" he asked, his eyes wide with expectation.

"Uh, well, no. We had just found the box when you signaled for us to come up." Will slipped the bullet into the net bag beside the gold necklace.

"Damn," he said, peering out toward the diving line float as if he might see something Will and Harley had missed.

"Okay, well, get back down there and get the rest of those coins, the wooden box I mean, okay?" His tone was softer, as if he was asking a friend instead of making them dive at gunpoint. Drury picked up a couple of shell casings from where they'd landed in the cockpit and dumped them into a plastic yogurt container that was filling up from his target practise.

"What is that, a coin of some kind?" asked Harley.

"Yes. It's a double eagle."

Drury answered their shrug by saying, "It was worth twenty dollars in its day. There should be … well, a bunch of them down there, so let's get back at it," he said, hurrying to switch their tanks.

"And today? How much is it worth today?" pressed Will.

"Uh, well, it depends, you know, on a lot o' things," Drury answered evasively. He left them to make their way to the Zodiac and back into their diving gear. He activated his cellphone and skipped along the side of the pilothouse to the massive aluminum mast.

The wind carried bits of his telephone conversation back to them. "It's me … They've found it … Well, okay, not all of it … some double eagles. Wasn't that what you thought he'd been paid with? Uh, dunno. Let me look …"

Drury pulled the coin from his pocket and scratched at it with his thumb before resuming his conversation.

"Looks like 1860, so that's the right time period, right? Oh, and there was a big metal case ... Well, I guess it could have been a crew member's money box. But I can't see the initials *P.B.* ... Dunno for sure, now do I? ... Well they're going to dive again so if you want to ... Sure. See you then." He switched off the cellphone.

Weighed down by their fresh tanks and weight belt, Will and Harley shuffled to the edge of the Zodiac, sat on the bumper and rolled back into the ocean. The water was warm but Will was glad for the wetsuit's insulation. Repeated dives tired them out and even warm water started to feel cold.

Halfway to the dive line, Harley spat out her snorkel. "Stay focused and stay alert. We may have to get ourselves out of this jam."

They both looked to the nearest shore, close to a mile away. Trying to get to it would make them easy targets for somebody chasing them in a Zodiac and with a gun.

They exchanged okay signs, then slowly descended along the dive rope.

Two tugs on the vacuum line got the compressor humming. As if realizing they were going to have to rely on each other, they each took hold of one side of the big hose and resumed vacuuming near the skeleton.

They uncovered what looked to be a muzzle-loading pistol, misshapen by the years below the sea. Will wondered if it was the weapon that had killed the man lying there. At least, Will assumed it was a man and not a woman who had been shot in the head, because seafaring at the time of muzzle-loading weapons was more of a man's trade than a woman's.

What they uncovered were day-to-day effects of the crew: bottles, broken or chipped plates, cups and such. They did not see any more coins. But they did find a wooden box with brass fittings on it. Salt water had fused the hinges closed. Because it had been under so much sand, it wasn't covered in coral. As the light played on its surface, Will thought he made out the letters *P.B.*, the initials Drury had told them to look for. Had they found the jackpot?

They heard the whir of an approaching boat. Will and Harley looked at each other before peering out of the gash in the hull, wondering if it might be someone who would rescue them. They swam out of the hull to see the boat above them tie up in the sailboat's lee just ahead of the Zodiac. The vacuum stopped and Drury called them up with two tugs. They dragged the box out so Harley could inflate the flotation bladder and float it to the surface.

Drury helped hoist their find into the bottom of the Zodiac, pumping his right fist with excitement. The man who had just arrived hovered near them to see what they'd found.

Drury slipped back down to the Zodiac and pried open the wooden box with the crowbar. "Empty," he snarled to the newcomer, who shook his head.

Harley whispered, "That's Bennett." The man walked toward them, cellphone stuck to his ear. He was of medium height, with pale gray eyes. The breeze tugged a few strands of hair away to reveal a bald spot at the back of his head.

They heard another boat approaching.

"Okay you two," said Drury, "go below to the front cabin and wait there for a bit."

They slipped down the hatchway. As they made their way forward, past her berth, Harley pulled a drawer open and scooped up some things she then clutched to her stomach. They could hear Bennett walking overhead toward the pilothouse.

"Close the cabin door," said Drury as they heard a boat approach.

Harley closed the door to Will's cabin. Then she emptied Will's toiletries from a plastic bag and jammed her passport and wallet into it. She waved for Will to hand his passport and wallet over. She double-knotted the tail end of the bag before slipping it into a zip-lock bag, then wedged it all into her wetsuit jacket under her armpit. Will did the same with the net bag containing the bullet and gold necklace.

"We may have to make a break for it," she whispered, as she craned to get a look through the small porthole at the boat whose motor slowed to within about thirty feet of the stern's starboard side. Will strained to listen to the voices but could only hear seawater dripping from their wetsuits onto the teak floorboards.

"Now, that's weird," she said, waving Will over to have a look.

The high-bowed Boston Whaler that approached had a strange-looking person at the helm. Despite the warmth of the Bermudian sun they wore long sleeves and long pants, and a wide-brimmed hat that prevented Will from seeing any of the person's features. The shirt's light material rippled in the breeze. But what chilled Will to the bone was the fact that the person's hands and face were covered in gauze just like in his dream.

The solo passenger at the helm was not a big person, but because they were seated, it was hard to tell how tall they were. And they would likely remain seated: at the side of the steering console was a wheelchair, folded and secured with rubber cords.

The Boston Whaler hovered about ten yards away. The visitor produced a cellphone and Will heard another cellphone on *Wavelength* ring. Bennett answered. A moment later the conversation ended. The Boston Whaler spun around. Its twin outboard motors churned a white-foam wake, raising the bow clear of the turquoise water as it headed back for shore.

Will and Harley cocked an ear toward the pilothouse. They heard footfalls as Drury and Bennett trundled into the galley that occupied the middle section of the motorsailer just outside their cabin. There was an awkward pause.

"So, what did he say?" asked Drury, his voice muffled by the closed door.

Bennett sighed. "He says," he paused to sigh again, "he says he wants us to make it look like an accident."

Chapter Four

The Escape

*Zodiac: An open boat with a large, inflatable bumper
around its periphery.*

Will and Harley froze, and exchanged a look. Harley slid the little
deadbolt in place on the cabin door, but Will had no doubt that it
would yield to Drury's big shoulders. He stood on one side of the
V-shaped berth and as quietly as possible unscrewed the wing nut
that secured the hatch cover, pulled the adjusting rod off the nut
and pushed the hatch cover open till it rested on the deck.

"What does he mean by 'an accident?'" asked Drury. "You
mean, like a diving accident, or something like that?"

"Keep your voice down," hissed Bennett.

"This is crazy. We weren't supposed to do anything to them
except get the boat back. Don't know about you, but I didn't sign
on to kill nobody."

Bennett sighed again. "Well, what do we do with them? Can't
let 'em go now till we know if those double eagles are down there.
Then, I don't know, keep 'em quiet till we get away, right?"

"What if those letters of yours were wrong? I mean, the box is
empty right?"

"The letters aren't wrong," said Bennett. "We found the boat.

Maybe Papineau took the coins off before she sank. Just gotta find 'em is all."

Getting through the hatchway in a wetsuit wasn't easy. But with a boost from Harley he cleared his shoulders and on her next push, Will was able to propel himself through, the wetsuit absorbing the smack of his bum against the deck. He cocked an ear but, not hearing anybody hurrying to get above deck, he reached down and pulled her out of the hatch.

They tiptoed on top of the cabin so as not to be seen through the portholes.

Bennett broke the silence below. "Okay, tell you what, let's get them to do one more dive. I'll go with them and we'll see if we can't find all of it and then we'll make a decision about what to do, okay? It's easy for him to say, 'make it look like an accident,' but we're the ones who'll have to get our hands dirty. I mean, damn, I approached him to find gold, not kill anybody, especially not kids."

Drury called out, "Okay you two, you can come out now."

Will and Harley stepped into the cockpit behind the pilot-house. They heard Drury rattling the locked door to the cabin and say, "Bloody idiots, watch yourselves or you'll catch it." Drury kicked the cabin door open.

"Where the hell are they?" screamed Bennett. He and Drury both spun to look to the pilothouse just as Will slammed that door shut and wedged an empty tank between the door and the step to the cockpit.

They heard cursing and footfalls moving to the door, which Bennett and Drury rattled and banged as the cousins scampered down into the Zodiac.

Suddenly, a shot was fired through the galley's porthole. The bullet pinged off one of the aluminum shafts holding the Bimini in place. They ducked and looked back. Unable to aim at them through the porthole, Drury again battered the cockpit door.

The keys weren't in the Zodiac nor in the Boston Whaler Bennett had arrived in. They'd have to swim for it. But Drury and Bennett did have the keys and, judging by the splintering sounds coming from below, they'd be at them momentarily. As Harley skipped down the ladder to the Zodiac, Will smacked the yogurt container, sending the shell casings flying into the cockpit.

The cousins hurried into their diving gear. Will slipped a rigging knife from the Zodiac's console into his vest pocket. He looked up as the cockpit door yielded with a spectacular crash of shattering wood, followed by powerful kicks as Drury cleared enough of a path to reach the tank. It clanked as it was tossed out of the way.

Will and Harley looked up just as Drury's head and gun appeared above the cockpit's coaming. Drury screamed as he skidded on the brass casings. When his feet flew out from under him, he accidentally squeezed off a skyward shot just before his head smacked varnished wood.

"Drury, Drury, wake up. Are you okay, Drury? For God's sake," barked Bennett. His head popped up to look at them, his right hand covered in Drury's blood. A bloody-faced Drury staggered to his feet and gawked at them with unfocused eyes.

Harley untied the Zodiac's stern line but before Will could untie the bow line, Drury let off another shot that whizzed over their heads and through the blue Bimini cover. Will pulled two tanks free to roll around on the bottom of the rocking boat.

Harley jammed extra lead weights into their respective BCDs, then, each holding a spare tank, they toppled back into the ocean. Two bullets zipped through the water above them.

As the second bullet lost speed and tumbled to the ocean floor, Will swam to the Boston Whaler's bow and surfaced. He grabbed the bow line with his left hand, slashing at it with the knife in his right. On the third stroke it yielded and he fell back into the water.

Before he could cut the stern line Drury had pulled the Boston
Whaler close to the Zodiac while Bennett scanned for the two
runaways.

A howl filled the air as Drury hopped around the Zodiac on
one foot, his face contorted in pain.

"The tank. The damn tank broke my toe. Holy crap it hurts."

Will surged forward with a kick of his flippers. His left hand
broke the surface, clamped the Boston Whaler's stern line and cut
it with two quick knife swipes.

Above him, Bennett leaped from the Zodiac to the drifting
Boston Whaler and cleated it to the stern. It wouldn't take them
long to secure the two boats and resume their chase.

Will swam over to *Wavelength*'s anchor line and let himself sink
from sight. He stopped at a big shackle pin and used his knife's
marlinspike to unwind the wire that secured it. He then placed
the tip of the marlinspike into the eyehole of the pin, and gave it
a jerk.

As soon as the pin came loose, the nylon line in Will's left hand
jerked him upward and he banged his head on the boat's keel. He
fought to stay conscious as he closed the knife and pocketed it.

Will let more air out of his BCD, watching the rope of bubbles
floating up and giving away to anybody looking where he was and
where they were headed.

He felt a tug at his flipper and looked down to see Harley's
concerned face. Will pointed to his head, banged his right fist into
his left palm and pointed to *Wavelength*'s keel so she'd understand.

They looked up as the Zodiac's motor roared to life, then
reversed as their captors tried to keep the big sailboat from the
nearby reef, which kept them too busy to chase or shoot their
fleeing prisoners. Harley gestured for the knife and used it to cut
a length of the dive line, which she used to tie the two spare air
tanks together. This way she could pull them along with just one

hand. With a headache settling in, Will didn't argue about dragging his own spare tank.

Because bubbles would betray their location, she led Will to the gash in the wreck. With the flashlights from the net bag, Harley steered them over the skeleton toward the distant pool of light.

The swim took them over and around protrusions that occasionally clanged against the spare tanks in the wreck's tight quarters. Will's dull headache robbed him of focus so he struggled to stay alert.

The light at the far end of the tunnel came from another long tear in the steel hull. It was likely that the boat had wedged itself between two reefs, carving openings on both sides, which meant that water had probably flooded in so fast that most of the crew had had little time to get away. He waited for Harley to go through first and saw the vessel's twin screws. So this boat, whatever it was, couldn't be that old, because sail or a paddlewheel hadn't powered it.

Harley pushed her spare tanks ahead and sank low enough to get through sideways, this gash not being quite as wide as the one on the other side. She waved Will over. He was almost through when he felt a sharp pain as the hull's ragged edge slashed through the neoprene and released a cloud of blood from his left forearm.

He wondered why he didn't feel more pain. Perhaps the shock or maybe the salt water had numbed him. He clamped his right hand over the cut and squeezed it. Harley signaled for him to hold it there. She pulled the rigging knife out, cut her own neoprene sleeve, and peeled it off. She got him to push his arm through the sleeve and she held it in place. She cut a length of the nylon rope to snug up the extra sleeve to stop the bleeding.

Harley pulled his gauges forward to show him he was below a thousand psi. He looked at her gauges and wasn't surprised to see she was still above two thousand. Will knew he was an "air pig."

Harley had told him it was perfectly normal for first time divers to consume more air. Normal or not, at this rate he wouldn't have enough to get to shore. He would have to surface and that would give their location away to Drury and Bennett. He was determined not to betray her position, even if it cost him his life.

Harley glanced at her compass before waving in the direction of a purple fan coral. When they got to the fan coral he was just above empty so Harley swapped his empty tank for a full one. She tucked the empty tank beneath a ledge so it wouldn't float up and give them away.

They had been swimming for what seemed like forever when they came upon another reef, which caused the ocean to foam around it. Will saw broad scrape marks where boats had scarred their hulls.

Harley led them around the reef before peeking to see what was going on with Drury and Bennett. They held on to the ledge to make sure they didn't bob up too high. A wave crested as it washed over the reef. As it flowed past them in a roil of white foam, they saw that *Wavelength* was now at a safe mooring.

Because of the distance, they didn't need to dive quite so deep as they made for a beach that could be reached by a set of stairs leading from the cliff top. One last look over their shoulder, a check on their compass bearing, and they sank below the reef's warm ocean spume.

They kept swimming till Harley ran out and swapped her tank, jamming the empty one inside a phantom fishing cage lying on the bottom. On her signal, they did another surface check. Bennett and Drury were zigzagging the Zodiac toward shore, peering over their respective sides for the escaped divers and for reefs that could damage their hull and propeller.

They slipped back under the surface when Will's air ran out.

Chapter Five

The Stonecutter

*Tender: The small boat used to get from shore to ship and
tied up with a line called a painter.*

Will fought off a moment of panic as he grabbed Harley's emergency regulator and, after a few calming breaths from her tank, they swam in tandem. When they both ran out of air, Harley let their gear sink to the bottom. The big, rolling waves hid them from Drury and Bennett's searching eyes.

Turning shoreward, they both spotted a man sitting effortlessly on the ocean's surface. The second man from Will's dream, the one with the sad eyes, waved them closer. Will shook his head to make sure he wasn't imagining it.

He was a broad-shouldered black man, flashing an encouraging smile and flicking his left hand to bring them to him, to safety. But instead of the long blond curls Will had seen in his dream, the man wore a bleached straw hat with frayed fringes that fluttered like long, blond hair. He held a slice of orange in his right hand.

A wave pushed them within a few feet of the big man who stared at them, then at the Zodiac. Will threw a frightened look over his shoulder. The man's powerful, long arms pulled Will and Harley behind him into a circular coral formation where the water appeared to boil.

They hid behind his broad back and the wicker basket that held his sliced oranges. Sitting on the edge of the coral made him look like he was sitting on the ocean's surface.

The Zodiac was within thirty yards of them. Taking the initiative, the man held up a couple of slices of orange and waved them at Bennett and Drury. "You want some orange? It's some good. Been soaking here since morning. Nice and cold. You won't get none better."

Peeking out from behind the wicker basket, Will and Harley saw Drury and Bennett exchange a look before staring out to sea where a fishing boat was winding its way. Drury reversed the Zodiac in a horseshoe turn, then rumbled off toward *Wavelength*.

"They moving away some, but best you two stay put a bit till it's safer."

The Zodiac picked up speed and the fishing boat thrub-thrubbed closer to Will, Harley, and the man on shore. Her captain eased the throttle back and held about twenty yards from them.

"Well shut my mouth wide open, if it ain't Aubrey Dill, in the flesh," the white man called out. "What you doing out here sitting on the boilers with an incoming tide, Aubrey? Won't make getting back to shore none too easy, now, right?"

Their savior just nodded.

"Say, why don't I let the tender float in and give you a ride back?" After a moment, he added in a voice tinged with sadness, "Come on now, Aubrey. Nothing good's gonna come from you staying out here. You being my best friend and all, you know I'd never get over it. No sir, no sir." He sounded as though he was from the American South.

"I got some young friends here might need some assistance,

Sherman. If you're not too particular about your help."

That seemed to be all Sherman wanted to hear. He pulled in his tender and pushed it toward shore and let out the painter. The tide and waves washed it their way. Aubrey Dill looked back at a pair of shoes on the shore.

"If those are yours, I could go back and get them for you, Mr. Dill," offered Harley, knowing Will couldn't swim any farther.

The big man stared toward the shoes in the sand as if making up his mind, then shook, yes. "Might as well get 'em back. Yes, might as well."

Harley steadied the bobbing tender so Will and Aubrey could climb in. The tender's bow rose in the air as he settled on the stern-most thwart. Harley dove into the water and did a head-up crawl to shore. Will wondered where she got the strength.

She did a one-armed sidestroke with the shoes held high in the other arm. She handed them to Aubrey and then hopped in beside Will. Aubrey pulled a watch out of the shoes, stared at it as if unsure of what to do with the unexpected time on his hands, then slid it back onto his wrist.

Sherman hand-over-handed them back to his fishing boat. It looked a bit like a Cape Islander, with its high bow and low sides. He had fishing rods in place as though he'd been too pressed for time to put them away. On either side of the boat was an outrigger.

He gave Will and Harley a hand up, but Aubrey ignored his outstretched hand and, in one graceful motion, stood in the bottom of the tender, swung his long left leg over the fishing boat's gunwale, and flexed his right leg till he was safely aboard, nodding a thanks Sherman's way.

Aubrey took the painter from Sherman's hand and together they hoisted and secured the fiberglass tender onto the foredeck, making sure not to block the hatch. This was obviously not the first time these two had been on this boat together.

Sherman clambered up to the flying bridge and moved the throttle forward. The diesel made the big boat quiver. Aubrey opened a cooler with a sun-bleached blue cover and fished out four bottles of water. He handed one to Will, one to Harley, and called up to Sherman before tossing him one, then sat down to twist the top off of his and take a long, slow pull from his own bottle.

Will couldn't help but stare at Aubrey and wonder about this recent turn of events. Harley unzipped the jacket on his neoprene diving suit, then gestured for him to drink some water. People on the water often forget to drink because they are surrounded by water, but it is essential to hydrate when scuba diving. Will drank half of his bottle as he slumped on the mall bench, careful not to snag his head on the sharp hooks hidden behind the multicolored lures that hung above him.

He turned his face to the afternoon sun as Sherman maneuvered his boat through the reefs with obvious knowledge of the Bermuda coast. There was something comforting about watching a good sailor practice his craft.

Wavelength had disappeared. Will stood and searched around but could only see a few boats too far off in the distance to tell if one of them was their recent prison. Harley stood beside him looking.

"Well they sure moved off in a hurry, now, didn't they?" she chortled with relief.

They chugged on for what seemed an hour as the sun lowered in the impossibly blue sky. They were in a harbor now, so Sherman slowed so as not to create a wake. Aubrey tossed two bumpers over the starboard side and when Sherman nudged up by the dock he cleated the stern line, Harley the bow.

Sherman hopped on the dock, gave the attendant his credit card, and, without a word, skipped off. Just as the attendant finished refueling the second tank, Sherman came back with four packages in his hands. He stepped on the gunwale, then down to the cockpit and handed out the warm packages to everyone. He put his own down on a big container Will assumed stored caught fish. A steady drip of cold water ran down one of its rusty metal legs and out to the nearest scupper. Probably from the ice Sherman uses to preserve his fish, thought Will as he unwrapped the package.

It was a sandwich with a thick layer of thinly breaded fish covered in tomato wedges, lettuce, and a smear of mayonnaise on one slice of bread, and mustard on the other. He hadn't realized how hungry he was till he bit into it.

"Can't believe how fresh this tastes."

"Should be, I dropped that grouper off not three hours ago," said Sherman, wiping a fleck of mayonnaise from the corner of his mouth as he smiled.

Aubrey stared at his sandwich as if unsure he wanted to eat it. As sighs of contentment filled the cockpit, he unwrapped and ate his too.

"So," started Sherman after sipping his water, "how'd you three end up together out there on the boiler?"

"The boiler?" asked Will.

"The circular coral formation that makes the ocean inside it look like she's boiling. How'd you come to be there with Aubrey?"

Will was surprised that nobody had thought to ask him about it earlier. Perhaps they had bigger issues on their plate than two teenagers in wetsuits washed up on a Bermudian beach.

Harley explained that they had believed they were delivering a sailboat to Bermuda until they'd been held at gunpoint and forced to dive for something, on a wreck.

"This guy Drury pulled a gun?" asked Sherman.

Harley nodded. "He wanted us to find a wooden box that was supposed to be full of double eagle coins from 1860."

"Well, if those coins are from 1860, it sounds to me like a Civil War blockade runner," said Sherman. "Don't recall there being a known wreck off o' where I picked you up. The *Marie Celeste* is the best-known blockade runner that sank here in Bermuda."

Will was too tired to ask what a blockade runner was. Sherman continued, "'Course, fisherman an' divers keep finding unknown wrecks all the time. You want me to call the police for you? Nobody should be pointing guns and kidnapping people, no sir, no sir."

Harley said, "Uh, actually, we're going to be staying at Windy Farm and —"

"That's Dr. Doan's place," said Sherman. He took off his dark sunglasses, which were so broad they looked like a welder's mask. Will was startled by how white his skin was behind the sunglasses.

"Yes, Marianne — Dr. Doan I mean — is expecting us. Her son Yeats goes to high school with me. Or at least, he did last year, in Halifax. We left our arrival a bit loose to allow for uncertain sailing times, so I think I'd like to talk to Marianne about what to do next."

Sherman nodded as he balled the sandwich wrapping paper and dropped it into a big plastic barrel garbage can.

"Oh, for sure. But it's getting late. Why don't you stay the night with Aubrey at his place and he could run you up to Windy Farm in the morning? Right, Aubrey?"

Will had the strange feeling that Sherman wanted them to do him the favor of staying with Aubrey, instead of the other way around.

Without waiting for an answer, Sherman took his credit card back from the attendant, signed the receipt, and started his engine up.

"Wow," said Will, staring at the fuel pump. "Does that say five hundred dollars?"

"Yup. That's the max it shows, so I have to do it twice to fill this baby up. I go through anywhere from a thousand to twelve hundred dollars' worth o' fuel every three days I fish. And Bermuda dollar's on par with the US dollar so you know that's expensive. Now, you two okay with staying at Aubrey's place for the night?"

He threw a questioning look at Aubrey.

"Uh, well, I, uh, hadn't planned on having guests, but, I guess —"

"Perfect," said Sherman, opening the engine up as he headed through the harbor and back out to sea.

Will and Harley exchanged a quick glance. Anything was better than being captive on *Wavelength*. But Will sensed that Harley shared his feeling that something fishy was going on here, and not just because they were on a fishing boat.

Chapter Six

The Blockade Runner

*Blockade runner: During the American Civil War, President Lincoln
enacted a blockade of ports called the Anaconda Plan, to bring the
South to heel through starvation and financial ruin. The South
responded by calling on enterprising captains to run the blockade
for country and profit. Those boats and their crews that ran the
blockade were called blockade runners. The best boats were fast,
sleek and hard to detect.*

Sherman tied his fishing boat up to the dock behind Aubrey's
house. The first thing Will noticed in the evening light was how
tidy the property was. It was a modest bungalow, painted pastel
yellow with a high-peaked white roof. On the ride over, Will had
observed that all the roofs were white. Harley explained that all
the roofs had ridges that channeled rainwater down to spouts that
allowed each house to store water in large underground cisterns.
Keeping the roof clean and white meant that very little dirt built
up in the houses' drinking water. He asked her how she knew so
much about Bermuda's water system.

"Yeats told me about it. He told me all kinds of things about
Bermuda. He was born here." She saw the puzzled look on his face
so she continued, "Yeats is Dr. Doan's son. He was in my class last

year. He lived with his uncle, Dr. Doan's brother. We were, uh, we were, you know, friends, so we talked a lot. Me about Nova Scotia, and him about Bermuda. I told you about him, about the family we were going to stay with, remember?"

Harley had told him before they left Lunenburg that they were going to spend an extra week with the family of a class friend. He was pretty sure she hadn't mentioned his name and frankly, with the rush to take his diving lessons so he could scuba dive with his license, he was just happy to hear they had a place to hang out for an extra week.

Pastel colors seemed to be the order of the day in Bermuda. All the houses dotting the shoreline were in those muted tones. Even the sun seemed to follow that color coordination by using the clouds on the horizon to give its setting a pink hue.

They had barely walked off the dock when a big black Lab wiggled its way toward them, making throaty sounds of recognition as it rubbed up against Aubrey's legs as if it hadn't seen him in ages or, worse, feared never seeing him again.

"Yes, Hamlet," said Aubrey, rubbing the writhing dog between the shoulders, "I'm back, I'm back. No need to go on that way. I'm back."

But Hamlet carried on like that for another few moments while Will and Harley smiled as he squirmed up against Aubrey, desperate to confirm Aubrey's presence.

"Yes, yes, you're a good-looking beast, Hamlet. And what the world needs is more good-looking beasts. Yes, they do. Of course they do," said Aubrey, his voice encouraging the black dog to wag its tail harder.

Aubrey's dark suit was saline streaked from the salt water. Neither Will nor Harley had asked him why he was dressed that way while sitting on the edge of a coral boiler. The fact that Sherman hadn't commented upon it at all was really puzzling, but suggested it was not a question to ask.

They continued up the stone path to Aubrey's house. The plan was to get to Windy Farm tomorrow. Will and Harley carried their diving suits. Harley had peeled hers off. She helped Will roll his diving jacket off, cutting it at the elbow so it continued to protect his forearm. With that off he was able to shed the bottoms.

Sherman had produced a couple of old hoodies that he said he always kept onboard in case the temperature dropped. They were faded from sun and salt and had holes here and there, but they were definitely better than wearing neoprene, and tired as he was, Will would have been chilled without it.

Aubrey's house looked like nobody lived there. All the shutters were closed; the chairs around the garden table had been tipped so as to lean against the table like people did when they went away on a trip. Aubrey fished a house key from inside a flowerpot by the door and unlocked it. He told them to wait a minute and he'd turn the power on. Will wondered why he would have turned the power off if he was only gone a few hours. Perhaps it was a Bermudian thing.

Will flicked on a light switch but nothing happened. Aubrey made his way down the hall, opened a closet, and activated a breaker, which allowed the hall light to come on. Aubrey moved quietly and gracefully for a big man. Without breaking stride, he fingered a key off a hook by the door and crossed the few feet of driveway to the double door gate to the street. He unlocked a padlock and pulled a long chain from between the rungs of the gate. When he carried it back to the house, Will noticed it was a new chain and padlock, neither showing any signs of rust he was certain would accompany living so close to the ocean, as was the case for people in Lunenburg or Halifax.

Will saw that the small truck in the lane had been covered by a tarp. People in Bermuda sure closed up shop when they went out. Coming and going must be time consuming, thought Will. Sherman waved them inside and turned lights on as he progressed deeper into the house.

Aubrey had unplugged the TV and sound system and the empty fridge was unplugged and the door left open. Aubrey plugged the fridge's electrical cord back into the socket, which brought the light on till he hip-flicked the door closed.

"Were you going somewhere, Mr., uh, Aubrey?" asked Will.

From the corner of his eye he saw Sherman look to the floor as Harley shot him a "don't-go-there" look.

"So, let's have a look at that cut, shall we?" Aubrey said, ducking the question.

He untied Will's neoprene-covered forearm, which looked like a giant, trussed-up sausage. Will winced when the bits of rubber were pulled from the wound, which gaped open. It had stopped bleeding but he could see the edge of a white tendon. He knew from science shows that tendons were white but had no idea they were this kind of bold white.

"If you're going to wait till tomorrow to see Dr. Doan, we should close that wound up now," said Aubrey, pushing his chair back. He pulled a saucepan from under the stove and put some water on to boil. Here again he had to reconnect a utility, this time the main gas line by reaching to the wall behind the stove. Aubrey glided out of the room with the grace of a dancer in search of his partner.

A chorus of peeps that grew in intensity broke the silence. Sherman answered Will's questioning look by saying, "Tree frogs. We call 'em peepers. It's the male's mating call." Sherman studied a kitchen shelf covered in silver cricket trophies with Aubrey's name on them. Pictures hanging above the shelf showed Aubrey winning cricket tournaments or best player certification. Some of them showed Aubrey, who grayed with age as he continued in his winning ways, while the boy beside him in the pictures grew into a man. Will assumed this was his son.

Lowering his voice, Will asked Sherman, "Do all Bermudians leave their houses like this when they go out to the ocean? And what's with the dark suit in the water?"

Sherman shook his head and waved his hand at Will as if to erase the question that was hanging in the air.

Harley put her index finger to her lips to shush Will just as Aubrey came back into the room. It really was amazing how a man that big could walk so lightly. He had a long strand of dental floss, which he dropped into the boiling water along with a curved needle.

Aubrey filled a little bowl with hot water and sprinkled salt in it before he turned to the sink and scrubbed his hands twice before drying them. Then he produced a box of latex gloves from a drawer, pulled on a pair, and handed another pair to Harley. He waved Will over and had him hold the gashed forearm above the sink, then poured the saline solution into the wound.

"You were lucky you did that in the ocean. The salt water helped disinfect it. This is just an added precaution," explained Aubrey.

He patted the wound dry then sat Will down. He threaded the dental floss through the curved needle and, with the help of a pair of small, red-handled needle-nose pliers, drew the needle through one side of the gash, then the other. Will flinched as the needle nicked nerve endings. Aubrey tied a knot and had Harley put pressure on it with her gloved index finger before tying a second knot and cutting the floss. He repeated the procedure six times. Will really did look like Frankenstein's monster now.

Aubrey peeled his gloves off and took Harley's glove as well, which he carried out of the room. Will just stared at his forearm in amazement.

Sherman grinned and said, "Aubrey was a stonecutter for years.

Started helping his dad, then quit school at fourteen to work full time. Eventually bought the quarry out there," he said, wagging his thumb over his shoulder to indicate it was farther inland. "Didn't have cellphones back then. You or one of your mates sliced yourself open, best to know how to close that wound, 'r else you'd run the risk of bleedin' to death. Aubrey was a good stitcher if'n you needed one," said Sherman with a nod and a smile of pride by association.

Aubrey handed Will a glass of water and a bottle of painkillers and held up two fingers to let him know how many to take. Then he stood there staring at his kitchen as if surprised by the empty fridge when he opened the door. He closed it quietly, opened a cupboard and pulled out two cans.

"I could warm up some soup if anybody wants some."

"I best be on my way, Aubrey," said Sherman, pushing himself off the counter. "Fish biting early tomorrow. 'Sides, wouldn't do to show up an' not eat the missus's dinner, no sir, no sir."

Will leaned back in his chair and covered his mouth as he yawned. "Actually, Mr. … uh, Aubrey, that fish sandwich hit the spot and if it's okay with you, I'd just like to lie down. I'm awful tired after our long swim today."

Aubrey walked them down the hall and pointed to a bathroom. He stopped to pull out a fresh roll of toilet paper and to hang fresh towels on the empty rack. He then led them to a small, clean room with two beds flanking a side table. He turned the table light on and pulled sheets down from the shelf above the empty closet. Harley took them and thanked him before she hurried to make their beds.

Aubrey told them they'd find new toothbrushes in the bathroom medicine cabinet, and then walked Sherman outside.

Will opened the window a crack and could hear the peepers' chorus. Sherman and Aubrey walked past the window on the way to the dock.

"Gave me quite a scare there, Aubrey, you out on the boiler like that."

"Didn't mean to."

The peepers filled in the silence.

"I'm a shrinking man, Sherman. Everything I thought I was, everything I thought I'd made and built all disappeared the way Anthony did."

"Why the suit?" he asked in a lowered voice.

"It's the suit I wore the day Julie said she'd take me as her husband. I thought I'd wear it to meet her again after all this time. Hoping she'd be willing to take me back after what I did with Anthony. Or failed to do with him ..."

"You didn't do nothin' to — look, next time you feel like doing that, you give me a call and talk, why don'tcha? Me and the boys in 'a choir, we're all powerfully upset by what's happened to you and Anthony, you being a good man, a good friend, and a good father. No, don't you be arguing with me none, now, hear? No sir, no sir."

The peepers drowned out Aubrey's answer. Sherman started up his diesel while Aubrey cast the lines off and the boat chugged its way out to sea with its white, red, and green lights draining into the deeper darkness.

Will sat on the edge of his bed and fell sideways till his head hit the pillow. He struggled to pull his legs up.

"You didn't think that was all weird, him sitting there on the edge of the boiler in a suit? I just heard him say it was the suit he got married in. That's a strange one to come home with to explain, don't you think?"

"I don't think he intended on coming back, Will," said Harley in a hushed tone as she covered him with a sheet as though putting the matter to rest, at least for the night. But Will was focused on how the dream he'd had in *Wavelength*'s cockpit had been prophetic. He'd seen Aubrey before he met him and he'd seen the man wrapped in gauze holding four letters. In the dream he'd fired a gun at Will, a warning of the man's intent to have him and Harley killed and make it look like an accident.

Will was the seventh son of a seventh son. That had been the explanation given to him for his sensitivity to the paranormal. He was the only one to connect with the ghost of his great-grand-father, Bill McCoy, the famous rum-runner known as The Real McCoy who haunted the family schooner in Lunenburg. McCoy had called his awareness of the paranormal a gift. Some gift. His dreams usually scared him half to death. True, in some cases, those dreams opened doors. Would one of those doors explain the significance of the name H.M.S. *Lily* on the envelope blurring like it was under water? Before he could think any further, he was asleep.

Will woke with a start. He sat upright and blinked, taking a moment to remember where he was. The peepers mating call said Bermuda. In the distance he heard the low thrumming of a boat's diesel. It wasn't a boat passing because the sound was steady, didn't ebb.

He staggered to his feet, peered out the window to the ocean and froze. Just off the dock was a boat silhouetted in the moon-light, its white, green, and red running lights bobbing on the ocean. Had Drury and Bennett found them?

Chapter Seven

A Nocturnal Outing

*Boston Whaler: A light, sturdy, unsinkable boat
used commercially and for pleasure.*

The boat Will saw through his window was stationary. If Drury and Bennett were there why weren't they attacking? He turned to where Harley slept. Her breathing was regular and he didn't want to wake her unless he had to, not after she'd shouldered so much of the effort to get them away from *Wavelength*.

Will tiptoed out of the room and heard Aubrey's gentle snores. The man needed his sleep as much as Harley. So Will headed out the dockside door down to the concrete pier. If Drury and Bennett were on this boat, he'd yell and warn Harley. As he got closer, the boat moved in but not aggressively. It was only when he waved from the flying bridge that Will recognized Sherman.

"Sorry if I woke you, Will. I was just — well, couldn't sleep," said the fisherman.

"You worried about Aubrey? He's sleeping. So's Harley."

"Oh, good," said Sherman, his shoulders slumping with relief. "Hey, I'm up, you're up. So why don't I show you how pretty Hamilton Harbour looks at night?"

With Will aboard, Sherman moved off to deeper waters and

around the point of land that arced in protectively.

"Am I right in thinking that Aubrey was sitting on that boiler, hoping a big wave would take him off?" asked Will, hoping for an explanation that would make sense of things. "Why would he do that?"

Sherman's jaw twitched to the side as if he had trouble with the question. "A boat, a well-balanced one like mine here, sails through a storm just like she has for years, takes the best and the worst that the wind, water and skies can do to her, and keeps tracking until one day, this big wave comes along. A big, unexpected wave that slams her so hard that she staggers under the blow. Her load shifts and damages her structure, which causes her to list. Now that new reality robs that beautiful ship of all her grace. Well, Will, under those conditions, not all ships can right themselves or make it back to harbor, no sir, no sir. And that also happens to men on this ocean we call life."

Will didn't entirely understand but he did know that sorrow had damaged his own grandfather, had staggered him like he'd been hit by a big wave. It had taken a whole year for him to get back on track after his son, Will's dad, had died. Some assumed he wouldn't make it.

"I've been thinking about that wreck where we found the coins. Wouldn't there be a record of her sinking and of her cargo? I mean, a big ship like that must o' had a big crew and its sinking wouldn't go unnoticed, would it?" asked Will.

"There were a lot of blockade runners operating out of Bermuda back then. My great-grandfather being one of them. Good money to be made helping the South."

"I thought Harley said Bermuda and Britain had abolished slavery in 1834, so why would Bermudians help the South keep slavery?"

"Follow the money. Britain abolished slavery but she wasn't above letting her shipyards build and sell those sleek and fast

blockade runners, no sir, no sir. 'Specially not when you were paid
in cotton. With the blockade making it hard to get anything in
or out of the south, the value of tobacco and sugar went up, but
their biggest export, cotton, shot up in value because all the textile
mills in the American North and in Europe were starved for it.
Blockade runners would only accept payment in coin or cotton
that they could sell to the British or French for a small fortune.
Remember, Will, wars are fought for patriotism and profit. Follow
the money is what I always say."

"Did the same go for Bermuda?" asked Will.

"Well there were a lot of family links between Bermuda and
the Carolinas — we're on the same parallel. And with so many
new people arriving to run the blockade, cost of housing and food
here climbed out of reach, so people needed to make more money.
That included black and white Bermudians, 'cause money is a
color-blind magnet when you got to feed a family on an island
where the cost of food and shelter went through the roof. My great-
grandfather more than made ends meet as a blockade runner."

"I'm sorry, what are or who were blockade runners?"

"You know the Civil War in the US pitted the North against
the South over keeping or abolishing slavery?" Will nodded.
"President Lincoln implemented the Anaconda Plan, a blockade
meant to choke off trade that fed the people and the economy of
the South so's they'd give up their plan to break away from the rest
of the country. My great-grandfather served on boats that tried
to get around the blockade to bring the South goods that were
critical to its survival and — hang on!" bellowed Sherman,
throwing the helm hard a-port as a Boston Whaler cut across their
bow and roared past them. The man at the helm cursed and yelled
back at them, "Bloody idiots, watch yourselves or you'll catch it."

"That's Drury," blurted Will, recognizing both the voice and
the expression. "That's the guy who kidnapped us and shot at us.

Follow him," said Will, stabbing his finger at the receding boat.

"We wouldn't likely catch him even if we wanted to," said Sherman, trailing in the faster boat's wake. "No running lights on, so not much good goin' on, s'all I can say," added Sherman as he turned to stare after the boat that fled into the darkness.

Within minutes they were inside the harbor.

Sherman pointed to the dock where the now-lit Boston Whaler was tying up.

"Why'd he run without lights and then turn them on now?" asked Will.

"Probably didn't want anyone knowing where he'd come from. But in here, without lights he could cause an accident or draw the attention of the police marine unit."

Sherman handed Will binoculars. He trained them on the Boston Whaler and saw Drury scamper across the road in the direction of the big cruise ship way down at the other end of the dock, all lit up so you couldn't possibly miss that giant floating village.

Sherman brought them parallel to the dock. They saw Drury dash across the well-lit street, zigzag between tourists from the cruise ship, and disappear into a doorway wedged beside a colorful column. A second-story light came on. Will trained the binoculars on the second floor but the lit window had a set of blinds so he couldn't see anything.

The ride had chilled him and his teeth chattered. The hoodie and bathing suit weren't much to keep the ocean's coolness at bay.

"Best we get you home, Will," said Sherman, heading back out to the mouth of the harbor.

Will was so tired he didn't remember stepping off Sherman's boat or going back into Aubrey's house.

Chapter Eight

Windy Farm

Schooner: A sailboat with at least two masts,
with the foremast being smaller.

The next morning Aubrey pulled the tarp off of the small, white pickup truck with *Dill Enterprises* painted on both doors. He lifted the hood and reattached the battery cable. Nobody commented on the fact that undoing the battery cable wasn't the usual thing to do if you were planning to be away for only a few hours. Being in a left-hand-drive car took some getting used to, but was less surprising than the narrowness of all the streets. Aubrey explained that cars were not used in Bermuda till 1948. The petition to keep cars out of Bermuda had been signed by a lot of people including US President Woodrow Wilson and Samuel Longhorn Clemens, better known under his pen name, Mark Twain.

Because horses and carts had been the main means of travel throughout the island, the roads were extremely narrow for the cars that were now zipping along, almost all with scraped bumpers. On more than one occasion, Aubrey had to hug the outside part of the lane so that the side of the pickup and the mirror whacked the tall grasses and trees that leaned into the road at their peril. It was scarier when Aubrey had to skim the many stone walls that lined the streets, on one occasion actually scraping the side-view mirror because an oncoming car was too close to the center line.

The mood in the truck was quiet as Will and Harley searched the bays for *Wavelength*. They came to a roundabout near the city of Hamilton where a man with a straw hat was waving at all the passing cars. The man called out, "Have a nice day. God bless." He waved vigorously and smiled, his thin dark face framed by a bushy white beard. Will waved back, then Harley did, and they found themselves smiling at each other, then at Aubrey, who gave a small smile back.

Will looked to his right and saw a life-size bronze statue of the same man. He turned to Aubrey for an explanation.

"Johnny Barnes. Johnny was an electrician on the railway. For almost three decades now, he comes to this roundabout every morning, Monday to Friday, from four a.m. to ten a.m. to greet passersby. He's become an institution and citizens of Bermuda honored him with that bronze statue."

Aubrey took Harbour Road and drove for a few miles, then turned inland. At a big sign marked *Windy Farm*, Aubrey drove his pickup truck down the lane toward a mural. It was a portrait of a young ponytailed man hanging out from a tree. With his right hand and foot anchored to tree branches, he extended his left limbs to create an X as he overlooked Windy Farm below him. His left hand wore a falconer's glove and above him hovered a hawk with thin strips of leather hanging from its anklets. The lower right corner of the mural was signed *Yeats*.

"Those strips of leather hanging from the hawk's feet are called jesses, to secure the bird to its perch," offered Harley. They drove past a covered paddock, circled around to the parking lot, and came to a stop between two white lines that made sure you knew not to waste space. Bermuda was an island after all and space was limited.

Dr. Marianne Doan pulsed with energy. She caught Will's eye before Harley pointed her out. She had the same slim frame as Will's mother. She was tall and her long strides made her look even taller. Or maybe it was the riding boots. Her lips were tight with determination.

She had burst out of the office next to the horse stalls, heading to the covered paddock when she saw Aubrey's truck. Dr. Doan flashed a smile and cried out, "Harley, oh my goodness, you're here."

Harley sprang from the pickup and scooted over to give her a hug, which neither seemed in a hurry to end.

"Oh my goodness, Harley, you're even prettier than I remember. No wonder Yeats has been daydreaming since we got your emails saying you were coming to Bermuda."

"Yes," said Harley, winded from the strong embrace. "I'm sorry we didn't call you sooner, but we had a few bumps along the way. Oh, hey, this is Aubrey Dill."

"Oh, we know Aubrey. Hello Aubrey," she said, shaking his hand. "It's been a long while."

"Yes, it has," answered Aubrey with a voice so soft it was almost inaudible.

"Although we don't see him up here as much as we'd like, Aubrey is a long-time supporter of Windy Farm," she added, flicking a thumb to a plaque on the wall where Will read, "*This paddock has been generously provided by Dill Enterprises.*"

Dr. Doan took a step toward Aubrey and lowered her voice to say, "I was sorry to hear about your son. It must have been a terrible shock — I mean, the circumstances and all."

Aubrey nodded. "It was all of that. All of that."

"I see you came dressed for the beach," said Dr. Doan with a smile, eyeing Harley and Will's bathing suits under the hoodies.

"That's a long story. Oh, and this is my cousin, Will McCoy," said Harley, pulling Will forward.

"Hello Dr. Doan," said Will.

Will put his hand out and was surprised at her powerful grip. She held his hand and stared at the stitches on his forearm because he'd rolled his sleeves back. It was too hot for a hoodie but they had nothing but that and their bathing suits.

"You get those stitches here?" asked Dr. Doan.

"Uh, yes, yes I did —"

"What hospital stitched you up with …" she studied the stitches more closely, "I'm guessing that's dental floss?"

"Uh, yes it is, Marianne. But it wasn't done at a hospital," Harley explained. "It was Aubrey who stitched Will up after he cut himself while we were trying to make our way to shore. It's a long —"

Dr. Doan's cellphone rang in her pocket. It cracked Will up because it was the sound of a horse whinnying.

"Sorry, have to take …" said Dr. Doan, moving off a little before answering the phone. "Yeats is over there giving an archery lesson Harley. Why don't you go say hi?"

Harley waved Will to come with her and she skipped along the patio stones that ringed the horse stables all the way to a clearing. On the closest end was a group of about ten archers with four instructors who wore pale blue T-shirts that had *Windy Farm* written on their backs with the image of a horse staring out. About twenty yards into the clearing stood ten straw-backed targets, each resting on a solid tripod made of two-by-fours. Behind the targets was a forested section that seemed to go on for quite a bit.

As they approached, the students laid the notched end of their arrows on the string and when ordered, drew it back and let fly. Only the two instructors on either end actually hit with accuracy. The guy with the blond ponytail at the far right hit the red bull's-eye effortlessly. But judging by the euphoric clamor from the students, you'd think they had all hit the bull's-eye.

The participants put down their bows on the big table in front of them and the ponytailed instructor called out, "Clear." The participants walked single-file around the tables, to the targets and withdrew their arrows before returning to their respective shooting positions to repeat the process.

On the ride over, Harley had explained to Will that Yeats's father was a university professor in Maine, while his mother worked here at the therapeutic farm. Dr. Doan was a psychiatrist whose father, also a psychiatrist, had founded Windy Farm after a particularly violent hurricane had devastated the island and shaken many emotionally vulnerable residents who had no place to steady themselves. These were young people who already had physical or emotional challenges that had been made worse by the storm's battering. He'd built them a haven.

"Hi Yeats," said Harley, raising her voice to be heard over the archers' jubilations.

The blond ponytail swung around. The young man with a high forehead and a dazzling smile was the falconer pictured in the mural they had passed on the way in. He rushed over, scooped Harley in his arms, and twirled her around so fast she pulled her knees up and laughed. The way Harley buried her face in his neck made it clear to Will that Yeats was more than just a friend. The applause and cheers from the group of archers made that doubly clear.

Will's cheeks were hot and his stomach knotted. Who was this Yeats? Why was Harley so friendly with him? This wasn't just a school friend. Feeling lied to and angry, Will realized he was clenching his teeth as if reacting to a threat of some kind.

A whistle's strident calls made them all look to the parking lot where a small bus had just pulled in.

"Changing of the guard," explained Yeats.

One of the other counselors got the archers to put their quivers, bows, wrist guards, and finger guards down on the tables in front of them. They made their way to the bus as it was unloading the new "participants," as Yeats called them. Two of the participants gave Yeats a hug, but it wasn't the kind of hug he had shared with Harley. At the same time, cars were pulling in and disgorging a throng of blue-T-shirted volunteers who greeted the new participants by name with handshakes, fist bumps, and high fives.

Dr. Doan made a broad wave from across the way for Harley and Will to come to where she had rejoined Aubrey.

"I have a problem," she said, waving her cell. "Three of my volunteers, three sisters, called to tell me their car broke down. I need a lead and two side-walkers. Can I press you three into service for the therapeutic ride?"

"Oh, well, sure," began Harley, looking to both Will and Aubrey to be sure they were of the same opinion. Still rocked by the show of emotion between Harley and Yeats, Will remained sullen.

"Great. Aubrey, you take the lead; Harley and Will, you're my side-walkers. Yeats, please get them some boots from the stable and some shorts and T-shirts from the volunteer lockers."

Within moments, they were standing on the far side of the covered paddock, Will and Harley now in uniform blue T-shirts and shorts. Aubrey just pulled on a T-shirt.

The regular volunteers had moved their mounted participants in a cluster waiting to move out. A boy standing away from the group was fitted with a riding helmet and helped to step from the loading ramp onto the back of a cream-colored pony with a thick, Mohawk-like mane.

Dr. Doan adjusted the strap under the boy's chin and said, "Jason, your usual guides aren't here today, but Harley, Will, and Aubrey here are going to make sure you get to ride, just like you do every Tuesday, okay?"

Jason, a frightened-looking boy of about eight, didn't appear to Will like he thought anything was okay. The boy swiveled in the saddle, desperate to find somebody he knew and trusted, then let out a high-pitched wail. The other riders started to fidget and their caregivers tried to calm them down with soothing voices.

"Can one of you sing?" asked Dr. Doan. "One of the sisters always sings to him before they go out. Calms him right down." When Will, Harley, and Aubrey looked from one to the other to the other, Dr. Doan was quick to add, "Doesn't have to be beautiful, just as long as it's a song. Any song."

Without a word of warning, Aubrey started to sing "Amazing Grace."

Everyone, Jason included, froze and listened to the powerful voice that held them in place. Harley's mouth was open in disbelief.

Aubrey's voice resonated through his chest, through his feet, across the concrete pad and up through everyone's legs. Jason's pony nodded his head, echoing everyone's thought: Yes, more please.

Aubrey sang, "I once was lost, but now am found, was blind but now can see," and the eeee of the last word went right through Will and made the stitches in his forearm tingle.

Without waiting for the spell to be broken, Aubrey made a clicking sound with his tongue like a man used to working with horses. He didn't tug on the reins. Their pony was only too willing to follow this man with the golden voice. The more he knew this man Aubrey, the less Will understood him.

Will saw that the adult counselors were riveted by Aubrey. They moved their mounts toward Yeats, who suddenly realized his job was to lead and not to gawk, thought Will with a little smirk. Yeats spun on his heels, opened the gate, and led the caravan of riders.

After about an hour's walk on well-trodden paths through the adjacent woods, they came back to their starting point where the children dismounted, Jason last. He strode down the ramp and ducked under the railing till he came up to Aubrey. Without saying a word, Jason took his hand and allowed the older man to walk him silently to the waiting bus.

Dr. Doan sidled up to Aubrey, leaned in, and spoke to him in a voice so quiet only he could hear. Other than a slight head tilt in Dr. Doan's direction, nothing indicated he was even listening because he watched the bus make a wide arc through the parking lot and turn at Yeats's mural as it entered the lane that ran along the length of the property.

Only when it had curved onto the road did Aubrey turn to Dr. Doan, purse his lips, and give her a slight nod in agreement to whatever she had proposed.

A bell clanged from the two-story building that flanked both the open-air paddock and the archery range. The volunteer counselors broke into animated conversation as they moved to the lower floor.

"Lunch," was all Yeats offered as explanation as he waved for Harley and Will to follow the mass of hungry people.

Aubrey excused himself, saying he had things to do. Will and Harley stared at him. "I'll be okay. We'll talk later," he said with a soft smile before driving off.

After lunch, some of the volunteers headed home, while others went to the stable to help clean the stalls.

Dr. Doan held Will and Harley back to explain what was going on. She was a little surprised to see that they'd arrived with no luggage. Harley gave her a brief account of how they thought they were just delivering a customer's boat, how they'd found some gear that turned out to be wreck-excavating equipment illegally smuggled into Bermuda. And, of course, that they had been forced at gunpoint to dive for an unknown wreck they weren't sure they could find again and without a clear idea of what they had been looking for.

There was a long pause while Dr. Doan, her elbows splayed, rested her chin on her clasped hands. She excused herself to make a call on her cell. She walked a few feet away where she got into an animated conversation with someone before she came back.

"Well," began Dr. Doan, "that was, uh … well, we'll call him a friend at customs who says there is no record of a Mr. Bennett coming and signing for any boat. Now, if you want to involve the police, and I can understand why you would want to do that, to find these, these criminals, well then, you're likely going to have to have one of your parents fly down here. Will is a minor and though you had a letter from his mother letting you be his temporary guardian, it disappeared along with the boat."

Harley was about to say something when Dr. Doan put her hand up to stop her. "I'm not calling into question your judgment or your conviction and courage, Harley. What I am saying is that you're seventeen years old. You have a letter you can't produce from your parents allowing you to embark on what should have been a fun trip, not a kidnapping. That's a very serious charge. If you report these facts to the police, I'm fairly certain they will insist that at least one adult member of your family show up and maybe even one adult for each of you. Remember, Harley, you signed the customs declaration. The authorities are likely going to be quite attentive to that point."

Harley shook her head. "That's ridiculous. We had no idea —"

"Be that as it may, that's likely how it's going to unfold, according to my … source," she said, nodding to her cellphone lying on the table.

Will shook his head. "We can't call either my mother or my grandparents because they would want to fly down here and help us. They're just finally getting together to talk things through after my father's death. We can't interrupt that. I won't interrupt that," said Will, folding his arms to show his determination. He turned to Harley for support.

"Uh, well yeah, I mean, no. That would mean Uncle Emmett. If he has to come, he'll have to close the sail shop. They're just getting the loft back on its feet after a few years of shaky financial, well, problems. So no, we can't call home."

Will nodded as if that made it final. He stole a glance at Yeats who seemed riveted by every word Harley said. That was starting to really annoy Will, who blurted to Harley as if their predicament was her fault, "So what do we do?"

She blinked at his forceful manner, then, in a calm, measured tone said, "Well, I guess we're just going to have to figure out what the heck is going on. We need to find where *Wavelength* has been taken, prove Bennett does exist, and show that we were forced to dive for that wooden box. Once we have proof, then, and only then, will we contact the authorities."

"Okay," began Dr. Doan, "I'd suggest you two bike around the island's various marinas to look for *Wavelength*. Won't be all that easy to hide a large motorsailer. I'd suggest you start with —"

"Hamilton!" blurted Will, remembering where he'd seen Drury last night.

They all stared at Will.

"It's the capital, right?" he said. "Well, it's realistic to think that if it's a treasure we're looking for, they'd want to deal with an established person on the island, right? I mean, who knows who Bennett is, or if he in fact exists. But that guy Drury, he's local and the man they were reporting to, well, isn't he likely to be local too?"

Dr. Doan nodded. "Yes, he might well be local but he could be from anywhere on the island or even be an ex-pat living here. That said, why not start from Hamilton and bike around the various marinas?" She flicked her thumb toward the second floor. "We get a throng of university students, mostly studying psychology and sociology, who come to take over in the summer and give our regular volunteers a break. They won't be here for at least ten days. So, Yeats will set you up in the upstairs dorm. You can get them some clothes from the lost and found — don't worry, they're all washed. And when you're in Hamilton, you can shop for things like underwear, toothbrushes and toiletries, okay? Take two bicycles with locks and helmets and it's off to Hamilton with you. Good luck in finding *Wavelength*."

Her look as she left the table said they were going to need it.

Chapter Nine

The Archives

Archive: A place that holds historical documents related to a person, community, organization or nation.

The little cafeteria at Windy Farm had served up a big lunch. From a deep bowl, Harley had grabbed a couple of bananas and some oranges for their trip into town.

Their rooms were, in Harley's words, "Wonderfully spartan" — which Will took to mean simple and clean — and they were: each had a single bed, a bedside table and reading lamp and a small closet where Will had nothing to store away. Down the hall they found men's and women's washrooms with showers and laundry facilities.

On a hip-high wooden table between the men's and women's showers sat a spacious, white, thin-wired cage containing a large red and white parrot who rocked from foot to foot on his perch. A child had painted the name *Humbert* on a sign leaning on the cage.

Will stopped to watch the parrot crack a sunflower seed in his beak before rolling its black tongue between the shell halves to withdraw the seed.

"Hi. Is your name Humbert?" asked Will.

"You betcha," answered the parrot, leaning in to retrieve another seed.

"Do you belong to a one-legged pirate called Long John Silver?"

Humbert's second "You betcha" cracked Will up, especially as Humbert spoke in a human-sounding voice.

Harley called from down the hall to suggest they make their beds now in case they were too tired to do it upon their return. The lost and found bin, full from last year's group, had yielded a couple of backpacks and various shirts, shorts, pants and even new running shoes that were their sizes. They had the money from their wallets that Harley had had the presence of mind to take before they had fled *Wavelength*.

The bicycles available for student volunteers looked new-ish, but had rust dots here and there due to the salty air. Yeats took two from the bike rack and adjusted the seats. Will bristled when he saw him put his right hand on Harley's shoulder, his left hand lingering on Harley's on the handlebars.

Without saying thank you, Will pedaled away as fast as he could. He heard Harley laugh and call to him to slow down and wait for her but he just kept pounding the pedals down the lane and onto the road. A car honked at him because, in anger, he'd made the mistake of riding on the wrong side of the road.

He made the roundabout twenty minutes later. Perspiration yoked a dark pattern on his blue Windy Farm T-shirt. Johnny Barnes wasn't there to make him smile this time. He took a pull from his bottle of water and realized it was almost empty after the long, hot ride.

There was a small horseshoe-shaped marina opposite Johnny Barnes's statue but none of the boats were as big as *Wavelength*. Riding on the left of the road made it easier to scan Hamilton Harbour to his left, but, with so many boats in Bermuda, finding the one they were looking for was going to be the proverbial needle in a haystack.

He passed the dock with the enormous tourist boat he'd seen last night while chasing Drury. He continued down Front Street, past a policeman in his white uniform. The officer was on a stand that looked like a large birdcage and was having his picture taken with tourists as Will whipped up Queen Street and locked his bike. He swapped his helmet for a blue Windy Farm baseball cap and leaned against the wall at Brown and Co., where they were going to shop.

Harley arrived moments later, swung off the seat, and rode the pedal to a stop opposite him. She locked her bike to the same pole Will had used.

"Hey, what's the rush?" she asked, knuckling perspiration from her eye.

Will shrugged and didn't look her in the face.

"You hear about the horse who walked into the bar? The barman looked up and said, 'Hey why the long face?'" she said, laughing at her own joke. Will didn't even crack a smile.

"So what's up, Will? Why the cold shoulder all of a sudden? What's going on?"

"I might ask you the same thing."

"Okay, I'm not following. Is this about Yeats? Are you upset that I'm — that we're friends, or something?"

"You're more than just 'friends,'" Will said, raising his voice and leaning forward. "You don't hold hands with friends like that. Why didn't you tell me he was your boyfriend?"

Harley spun and leaned on the wall beside him.

"Well, to tell you the truth, I didn't know what we were anymore. We were going out in high school last year in Halifax. But when we came close to losing the sail loft and your grandparents' house, well, I told him that I wouldn't have time for a boyfriend and that it was best we take a break so I didn't hurt him. And besides, Will McCoy, I don't think you tell me everything that's going on in your life, now, do you? I think you've got some secrets that you keep to yourself, right?"

Harley didn't wait for an answer. "And Yeats was pretty upset about my decision and the fact that I wasn't willing to discuss it. So, I wasn't sure he would be happy to see me. I didn't even email him to ask if we could stay. I emailed his mom. Marianne said yes, right away. She said Yeats was keen to see me but I just wasn't sure what to expect. Anyway, why does that bother you that I have a boyfriend? Are you afraid that I'm not going to hang around with you?"

"I'm not afraid of anything. I don't like being lied to, is all."

"Hey, Will, you're my cousin. I'm crazy about you. Nobody's going to take your place."

Will sighed and slumped against the wall. Harley slid down beside him. "Hey, if it means that much to you, well, I just won't be Yeats's girlfriend. I mean it. I'll just tell him that, you know —"

"No. Don't do that. Don't tell him that I'm being … Uh, look I don't know what I'm being or why it upsets me to see you with him. But it does. Thing is, that's my problem. I'll have to deal with it. I think that with dad dying, Mom, Granny, and Granddad all being away, well, I don't know. When you jumped into his arms I just felt like you were leaving me behind. Like my dad left." He looked to the sky. "I guess that's pretty lame, huh?"

"Nope. Not really. Nobody wants to feel abandoned. You listen to me now, Will McCoy. There's no way I will ever abandon you. That clear, Mr. Worrywart?"

Will nodded.

"I want to hear you say it," she said.

"Mr. Worrywart," replied Will, unable to fight the grin pulling at the corner of his mouth. They pushed themselves upright and she clapped her arm around his shoulder, leaned her forehead against his, then headed inside Brown and Co. to get some things they hadn't found in the lost and found bin. The two of them looked like members of a team in their matching blue Windy Farm uniforms.

Twenty minutes later they came out. Harley's backpack was a lot fuller than when they'd gone in. She insisted they cross through Par-la-Ville Park, to a self-serve yogurt shop Dr. Doan had recommended. Inside, you pulled down on the big black handle to release the rope of frozen yogurt into your container. Will chose coconut and Harley got pineapple.

They went back into the park through the moon-gate where, Harley said, you had to stop under the archway to make a wish. Will thought about it for a moment. He wanted Yeats to disappear but decided to wish that Aubrey would be all right.

They walked past a pond full of big goldfish, which, considering their color, should probably be called red or orange fish. They sat on the edge and ate their frozen yogurt. After a couple of spoonfuls, Harley flicked an index finger to the public washrooms and excused herself.

Will took a deep breath of humid air and closed his eyes a moment, letting the cold yogurt melt on his tongue. He opened his eyes and stiffened. There, walking right past him, was Bennett. Will could have reached out and touched him.

Bennett looked deep in thought as he sucked on a cigarette and didn't recognize Will in his sunglasses and Windy Farm baseball cap.

Bennett clutched a black briefcase and hurried across the park toward Queen Street where Will and Harley had locked their bikes. Will looked around for Harley but, not seeing her, took another scoop of his frozen yogurt, dipped his finger in it, and wrote "Bennett" on the stone he was sitting on. He added an arrow to indicate which direction he was heading in, put the containers down, and gave chase. If Bennett was going to go back to his boat,

Will would find it so they could report it to the police. He hoped Harley wouldn't be too panicked to find him gone.

Will let three scooters roar past as he stood by the old Perrot Post Office before crossing Queen to Reid Street.

Bennett had a funny walk. His short legs pumped his knees high in the air as if he'd spent a long time climbing stairs and he leaned forward like he was fighting a headwind. As he strode up the street he rocked the briefcase under his left arm and trailed the cigarette in his right like somebody used to hiding a bad habit.

His particular gait made it easy for Will to keep track. Bennett swung around to see if he was being followed. Will ducked in behind a woman pushing a big baby carriage, peered over her shoulder, then scooted back out in pursuit.

His quarry turned left on Parliament Street, which was lined with grand old buildings. The harbor was on the right. So, he wasn't going back to the motorsailer. Perhaps Bennett was making a pit stop before going to the boat.

Bennett strode past a pale brown building that gave way to a more modern white building, recessed from the sidewalk. It had the uninviting name of Government Administration Building above the glass entrance.

Will mingled with people on the sidewalk till Bennett took the basement stairs. Inside, Will saw that it led to the archives. He tiptoed down as quietly as he could, taking little notice of the large black and white photo of Bermuda when it was serviced exclusively by horse and carriage.

The small archives section was busy. A professor was lecturing a dozen university students about looking up the cause of past deaths by searching the government books he was pointing to. Some of the students were in a glassed-in room reserved for rare documents, where Bennett had gone. Will stood taller and hoped he'd pass for a university student, a short one.

Bennett opened up his black satchel and pulled out an envelope. He reached over to a container and lifted cotton gloves, which he slipped on before taking a book down from the shelf and opening another that the archivist brought him. Bennett's phone rang. He peeled off the gloves, pulled the phone from his pocket and scurried out past the receptionist and into the hallway, muttering, "Sorry, sorry."

Will slipped into the glassed-in room, pulled on cotton gloves so he wouldn't stand out and wove his way around the students to where Bennett had put down his satchel. Will looked at the book, an album of sorts with the title: *Paintings by Edward James*. The other book, the one the archivist brought him, was a death register for August of 1864.

It was opened at a listing starting August 2, 1864, which recorded the name of the deceased, his or her cause of death and the name of the witness. On that day, one Wilhelmina Coots, aged eighty-one, had died of "natural decay," witness Alexander Coots, husband. A Zebulon Grey, aged eighteen, had died of yellow fever, witnessed by Sergeant Major Bowls, with the Regiment of Foot. Sergeant Major Bowls had also been witness to the death of Private Wilfred Wiles, also eighteen but from a "self-inflicted gunshot wound." Bermuda back then wasn't the paradise it was now.

Then Will found the entry for Papineau Benoit, aged thirty-nine, who had died of yellow fever, August 2, 1864 in Trotters' Trail, witnessed by Dr. Luke Blackburn. Will's hair stood on end. Papineau Benoit's initials were P.B., the same as ones on the wooden box from the wreck. And he had died during the Civil War. And just before they fled *Wavelength*, Bennett had said to Drury that Papineau's letters told the truth.

Will copied those notes about Papineau Benoit from the death registry onto a piece of paper from a little box on the counter for that purpose. In the hallway, Bennett wagged his right index finger for emphasis as he talked on his phone.

Will noticed that the envelope looked old because it was flecked with imperfections and wasn't bleached. It was addressed to "Lily Benoit on Hollis Street in Halifax, Nova Scotia." The sender had also written, "Delivered by hand" in the bottom right-hand corner and initialed, "P.B." Another chill ran down Will's back. In his dream, the gauze-covered figure had held out an old fashioned envelope with the name H.M.S. *Lily* and the ink had run as if under water like the wreck.

Will pulled the letter out. The sender had identified himself in the upper, left-hand corner of the envelope as Papineau Benoit, of Duke of York Street, St. George, Bermuda. But what made Will jump was the card folded into the letter. It looked like a business card but it had a black and white photo of a man with a big neck and dark hair who rested his arm on a wooden box with the initials P.B. — the box they'd found on the wreck.

Bennett was finishing up his call. Will slipped the photo and letter back into its envelope, then into his backpack. He darted over to the far corner of the room and absorbed himself in an ancient Bermudian sign that warned against starting grass fires by throwing lit cigarette butts from the train.

As soon as Bennett walked past, Will glided sideways out of the closing glass door, slipped in behind the students listening to their professor, and walked calmly down the hallway so as not to attract attention. At the bottom of the stairs, he glanced back to see the panicked look on Bennett's face as he realized his letter was missing.

Bennett sprang to question the receptionist, who pointed toward Will. As Bennett turned in his direction, Will shot up the stairs two at a time.

In the ground floor lobby he blurted, "Sorry," to the couple he crashed through as though in a game of Red Rover. He sprinted back to Reid Street, rounded the corner, and spun around for a one-eyed peek back down Parliament Street. Bennett flew out of the building and looked around, throwing his hands up in frustration. He dialed his cell.

Chapter Ten

Papineau Benoit

*Gombeys: Members of a dance troupe in the Afro-Caribbean
tradition, brought to Bermuda by slaves. Prohibited from dancing,
the slaves would wear masks and ornate costumes including,
tall, peacock-feathered headdresses, and brightly colored tassels.
They would then dance to loud music made with drums
and trumpets, while carrying whips, axes and bows and
arrows as part of a celebration still carried out today.*

Will slowed his pace on Reid Street and turned into the front
yard of the Rock Island Coffee Shop, between the white, un-gated
gateposts. Through the window he saw a metal sign on the coffee
shop wall. It was a painting of a woman with a 1950s hairstyle.
The caption read, "I haven't had my coffee yet. Don't make me kill
you." Will didn't want anybody to kill him, especially not Drury or
Bennett. He sat at an empty table. The adrenaline from the chase
had worn off. He was tired and his hands shook. He worried that
Harley was panicking in the park, but he had to sit and catch his
breath.

A green-yellow bird the size of a grackle landed on the branch
of a nearby bush. Two others followed and they repeatedly called
out what sounded like "Qu'est-ce qu'y dit?" — "What's he say?"

What does he say indeed, thought Will as he fished the letter out of his backpack. Why was Bennett doing research in the Bermuda Archives? Did this mean they hadn't found what they were looking for on the wreck? What was so special about the letter that he panicked when Will took it?

Will pulled out the envelope with "Delivered by hand" written on it, and studied the card with the black and white photo of Papineau Benoit. If he had died of yellow fever, then did that mean he wasn't the skeleton lying in the wreck with the bullet hole in his head?

The date at the top of the first page had faded with time, but he could make out "1862." The letter was handwritten in a short, precise, cursive style. Will stared at Papineau's photo taken over a hundred and fifty years ago, and wondered who this man was and who was Lily Benoit, to whom he was writing. Was she his wife or maybe his sister? For some reason it bothered Will to snoop in this man's past, so he unfolded the letter with respect for its age and great curiosity about the sender and recipient.

My Dearest Lily,

Although in St. George less than an hour, I hasten to write this letter as my friend, Captain Peters, sails for Halifax presently and I dare not miss this opportunity to bring you up to speed as regards my peregrinations. He has promised to have this letter delivered to you personally, either at home or at the Halifax Hotel.

Will remembered his grandmother, a retired teacher and Scrabble wiz, using the word peregrination, which meant long travels and was derived from the well-traveled peregrine falcon. She had pointed to one flying by their seaside house in Nova Scotia. He missed his granny's apple crisp. Will chased away a feeling of homesickness and focused on the letter.

We had a most unfortunate incident while on our most recent
expedition. A US gunboat pursued us when I snuck the Almira up
the Cape Fear River. A musket shot was fired, the bullet striking a
metal collar on one of our spars. The ricochet broke my tibia. That
was extremely lucky because he was shooting the new and lethal
Minié bullet. A direct hit would likely have carried off my leg.

Will looked up, wondering how a man with a broken leg can
think himself lucky. He ignored the sounds of traffic rumbling by
on Reid Street. Suddenly he heard Bennett scream, "There he is!
Stop, stop! It's him, the McCoy kid! He's got the letter! There, at
the coffee shop."

Will sprang to his feet to see Bennett on the back of a scooter,
pointing at him. The scooter wobbled as the driver fought to
keep his balance as Bennett shifted his body this way and that
to keep Will in sight. The scooter smacked a truck's bumper with
a thump that made people on the sidewalk jump. The truck driver
yelled down from his window as Bennett hopped off.

The scooter driver veered over to the curb, pulled it onto its
center stand before swiveling to look at Will. He yanked his black
helmet with the red fringe on top off his head. It was Drury,
flashing a smile that held no kindness. Will's jailer glanced at
the truck bumper, waved the driver off, and sprinted in Will's
direction.

Will jammed the letter back into his backpack as he sprinted up
the stairs and through the blue door, looking for a hiding place.

He burst into a large room full of comfortable seats that didn't
match. A half dozen people sat reading from newspapers, maga-
zines, laptops, and tablets. Will looked up, but saw no place to hide.

He dashed into the room to the right, past two women busy
making teas and coffees in a room full of the fragrance of baked
pastries.

Will sprang out the back door and clattered down the stairs and across a patio and fled into a room through open double doors on the other side. A woman, surrounded by huge bags of coffee beans piled here and there, poured some into a large coffee bean roaster.

Will ran past her only to discover that the back room on the left was a dead end. He ran back outside to the big galvanized gate on the harbor side but it was locked. He could hear Drury's footfalls in pursuit.

Will yanked off his blue Windy Farm baseball cap and tossed it through the bars. It helicoptered its way to the galvanized walkway that led down the side of a building and to a lane that sloped away to a harborside road.

Will charged back into the roasting room, hoisted a half-empty jute bag of coffee, plunked it on top of a full one, and crammed himself into the tight corner nook he'd just made, tucking his knees to his chest, hopefully out of Drury's sight. But he wasn't out of the woman's view. She gave him a confused look.

Will jabbed his index finger in the direction of the sound of two people pounding down the stairs in pursuit, then pressed it to his lips and gave her his most beseeching look. She turned so as not to give his position away.

A second later, Bennett ran into the room.

"Excuse me," said the woman, wiping her hands on her long, coffee-stained apron. "This area is off limits to customers. Staff only, thank you."

"Bennett, c'mere," roared Drury from the patio.

Will scrunched himself forward and peeked through the window's thin coat of coffee dust. Drury was pointing at Will's Windy Farm hat lying on the walkway.

"He jumped the fence. I'm going to follow this way. You go back outside and circle around to see if you can spot him. Yell if ya do."

Bennett turned around and clattered back up the steel stairs into the coffee shop. Drury pulled himself onto the galvanized railing. He yelped as his foot slipped and he almost fell twenty feet to the concrete pad below. He caught the railing and threw his leg over, then dragged himself around, scooping the Windy Farm hat as he dashed down the stairs leading to the alleyway.

The woman had been watching everything in the reflection on the roaster's stainless steel casing. She turned and waved Will up.

"They're gone. Take the passageway at the far end of the patio. The door will open to Reid Street. I'd go left, toward the park if I were you," she said in a conspiratorial tone, nodding her support, having apparently decided that Will was the good guy.

Will let out a sigh of relief, pulled himself up, gave the roaster a wave of thanks, and bolted for the passageway to the street.

The blue door opened onto the same front patio where he'd been sitting a few minutes ago. From his backpack Will pulled Sherman's old hoodie. Despite the temperature, he slipped it on to hide the blue T-shirt that would give him away.

He moved at a brisk pace past Drury's scooter but forced himself not to run down Reid Street and draw attention. Will waited for the light to change at the corner. He sidled in front of a slow-moving man with a cane to have a look back — neither of his pursuers was in sight.

At the entrance to the park, Will again spun around to see if he was being followed. Two powerful arms slammed into him from behind and pinned him. He was caught. His knees buckled.

"Will McCoy, what on earth has gotten into you to disappear like that? Are you completely crazy?" shrieked Harley, who had twirled him around. "You don't like Yeats, that's fine. But don't you ever pull a little hissy-fit like that again and, damn it all Will, you scared me. Really scared me. I thought —" She stabbed his chest with her finger and he could see she was near tears and unable to finish her sentence.

His message scrawled in yogurt had faded in the bright sun. All Will could do was pull her into the park and away from sight.

"Harley, sorry, sorry, really, I, they, those two, they, oh, wow. That was close," he blurted, stopping to catch his breath.

He grabbed her hand and pulled her across the street to where they'd locked their bikes. He flicked his thumb up Reid Street.

"I saw Bennett walking across the park and wanted to follow him to the boat so we could, you know, call the police with proof that we — well anyway, he didn't go there, to his boat. He went to the archives, doing research I think is related to the wreck we were diving on. They were chasing me. Bennett and Drury. I just left them two blocks that way. Drury's got a scooter and I don't want to be anywhere near him. I don't know if he's crazy enough to pull a gun in broad daylight but I don't want to find out, do you? Now go. I'm right behind you."

Harley frowned, peered down Reid Street, not looking the least bit convinced. She whipped her keys out, unlocked her bike, and pushed it down Queen Street and across Front Street past the uniformed officer who was posing with a new group of tourists.

Harley turned left before hopping on and pedaling with Will right on her heels.

Will picked up the pace, passing Harley to lead them into a car park that ran along the water. The cars shielded them from view as they headed back out of town. Harley's face was set in angry determination. That was fine with Will, as long as they got away.

At a big pavilion by the water's edge they heard very loud drumming, whistles and horns blowing. They coasted to a stop and pushed their bikes to the edge of a raised, tented area where a dozen costumed people were running and jumping in front of a throng of tourists. The performers were dressed in costumes made up of strips of fabric in bright pinks, blues, greens, and yellows. They wore tall hats made of feathers and had masks that hid their faces, which made it all a bit spooky.

Will and Harley heard a woman call to her husband, "Come on honey, the Gombeys are performing." The Gombeys? What on earth are the Gombeys? wondered Will as he pedaled, hoping Harley would calm down once they reached Windy Farm.

Dinner at Windy Farm wasn't as boisterous as lunch had been. Harley was still upset with him and wasn't very talkative. Yeats looked upset because she had removed his hand from hers. Well good, thought Will. Now he knows how I feel.

Will volunteered for kitchen clean up. When he had finished, Yeats told him Harley had gone to bed. Will saw the light on beneath her door, but decided against trying to explain things further till the morning.

The shower he took made him feel much better. He said, "I sank some boats and set fire to the port today, Humbert."

The parrot answered, "You betcha." He slept in a pair of running shorts with the mosquito net overhead. He was anxious to read the rest of the letter but promised himself he wouldn't get into it until he could share it with Harley.

He would have had a peaceful sleep if it hadn't been for the dream he had about Papineau Benoit's fight.

Chapter Eleven

A Confederate Town

*Patch screw: One of the first propellers made for ships that
succeeded the paddle wheel boats, powered by coal-fired steam.
John Patch of Shelburne, Nova Scotia tried to patent his design,
only to have it stolen and patented years later while
he died in debtor's prison in 1862.*

Will knew he was *having a dream because the man sitting back in
the barber's chair with his feet up on a stool was Papineau Benoit, the
same man whose picture was on the calling card.*

*The stocky barber was a black man with a light complexion and
huge sideburns that swept down his broad face like the blades of hockey
sticks and rested just above his chin. He finished shaving Papineau's
face with a straight razor, then retrieved a hot steaming towel from
the clay pot sitting at the front of the kitchen's fireplace, which gave
off an occasional crackle. He toweled off the last bits of shaving cream.*

*Papineau nodded to a notebook whose page was full of corrections.
"I see you continue to take lessons, Joseph." The barber nodded and
said, "It is hard for a man to be the author of his own destiny if he
can't read or write."*

*The barber's small hands snip, snip, snipped away with such speed
that they resembled brown butterflies hovering around Papineau's*

head. The captain read a letter and didn't look happy about its contents. He folded it and placed it on a nearby table.

The barber held the mirror up for Papineau and asked, "Everything all right, Mr. Papineau?"

"Disturbing news from home. But it pales in comparison to what the world is going through." He looked at his reflection in the mirror and nodded his approval, saying, "Yes, that will do nicely, Joseph. I sail for Charleston in the morning but will look in on you upon my return in a few weeks."

Joseph the barber spun the big cape off of his client's shoulder, shaking cut hair to the ground. Papineau pivoted his legs off the stool, standing up stiffly as he pulled coins from his pocket.

The barber swept the hair from around the spindled chair and, without looking up, said, "Now, Mr. Benoit, you know your money's no good in this establishment."

Papineau stacked the coins on the table by the letter, then adjusted his shirt and refastened the top button. The barber rested his broom on the wall so he could pick up the notebook, opened to a page full of spelling and grammatical corrections.

Nodding to the coins, Papineau said, "Remember, Joseph, you need to be treating Susan to an occasional delight. Man has to know how to treat his wife with a little indulgence now and then, isn't that right? Did I hear that Susan's making a dress for Georgina Walker? What wouldn't I give to be a fly on that wall?"

The barber let out a sigh and smiled as he nodded.

"At a dinner I attended, I heard Georgina Walker complain that black Bermudian women greet her as an equal," added Papineau as he pulled on his jacket.

"Well," said Joseph, brushing the jacket's shoulders, "She is married to the Southern Consul, and their stated purpose is to maintain slavery. Imagine that'd be a hard thing to do if you thought the person you kept in chains and whipped was your equal."

The door flew open and a frail man with a beard and a smock flecked in paint poked his stricken face inside. Speaking with a British accent he blurted, "Mr. Benoit, come quick, Villiers Rougemont and his men are attacking poor Mr. Allen. When he tried to stop them from cutting down the American flagpole, six men beat him to the ground. Please hurry, before —"

Despite his limp, Papineau sprang past the painter.

Rainey leaned into the fireplace, reached under the mantel, removed a brick, pulled out a small steel box and clinked the coins into it. He hesitated a second, then also stuffed Papineau's letter in the box before putting it back. Rainey tossed his striped barber's apron onto the table and charged behind, asking, "Where is he, Mr. James?"

The painter clapped his straw hat back on his head and scurried behind, yelling, "Over by Penno's Wharf."

Six men huddled around a man lying on the ground beside a flag-pole rising like a mast above the wharf. The men passed around a bottle of rum and laughed. The one with the ponytail was wound up to kick the stricken man when Papineau's thick hands spun the bully around.

Papineau tapped his broad, high forehead against the bully's then pushed him back, holding him at arm's length.

"Enough, Villiers. Take your hooligans and be off with you, d'you hear, man?"

The laughter stopped as the others watched Villiers Rougemont pull a small, double-barreled pistol from his jacket, cock the hammer, and jam it into Papineau's ribs.

"How about I blow your guts all over Penno's Wharf, Papineau?" hissed Villiers.

Joseph arrived and parted the cluster so he could tend to the fallen man. He yanked a handkerchief from his pocket, using it to wipe blood from the victim's forehead.

"You'd be charged with murder, Mr. Rougemont," said Joseph to *the gunman. "Shooting a blockade-running captain isn't the same as shooting a black man. 'Sides, you'll find a heap o' trouble from Major Walker if'n you kill one of his most successful captains. That's the truth of the matter."*

The painter pointed his hat at the gunman. "Local sympathies for the Confederacy won't save you from hanging if you pull that trigger. As God is my witness."

A policeman parted the farthest group of onlookers who had stopped at the dock to watch. Seeing him, Villiers slipped his gun back into his vest pocket, and smiled a crooked smile as he waved his drunken fellows away.

Papineau helped Joseph pull the traumatized man to his feet. "Are you all right, Mr. Allen?"

Despite his dark beard, the man looked pale and was so unsteady on his feet that Papineau and Joseph each draped one of his arms over their respective shoulders as they walked him away.

"They didn't get my flagpole this time," said Mr. Allen with a small smile.

"How did we come to this?" asked Joseph the barber, shaking his head.

"I will tell you, Joseph, how we came to this. We lost sight of the one element that makes America a great country," said Allen. "We have lost the ability to compromise and will be forever cursed as a nation until we recover that faculty. And our enemies will feast on our bones as we fight amongst ourselves."

"Come, let's get you home and I'll put the kettle on for some tea," said the painter as he led the way. He turned to Papineau and Joseph and whispered, "Somebody should take a straight razor to Villiers Rougemont's throat."

Will jerked awake and sat up in bed, his hand to his throat.

After breakfast, Will and Harley were asked to help exercise some of the horses boarded at Windy Farm. "The room and board charged to keep these horses helps defray the costs of running the center. We also sell the manure to local gardeners and grow our own vegetables to keep expenses down," explained Dr. Doan as they left their dirty plates on the counter and headed to the barn.

Inside, Harley grinned as she tapped a sign over the office door that read, "A woman's place is on a horse." On the office's inside wall hung a bow and arrows. The bow wasn't the kind the participants used. This bow looked like a curly bracket and had pulleys at either end. When used in tandem, pulleys, as Will knew from sailing, allowed the user to exert greater force than he or she expended. In this case, the bowman could pull the string back quite far with little actual effort. The system compounded the user's strength, hence the name compound bow.

It also had a carrier that held three arrows. But these weren't target arrows, unless the target had four legs and could find its way into an oven with baked potatoes, thought Will. The three sides to these tips looked razor sharp and likely not easy to pull out of a body on the receiving end.

Harley had taken riding lessons for a few years so she knew her way around a horse. Her mood had improved after a good night's rest.

Yeats showed Will how to tack up and mount a horse. He explained that it was mostly a question of balance, and that was achieved through the knees. They walked their horses through the open paddock because it was overcast and the sun wasn't that hot.

Will was shown how to hang on to the mane if all else failed, a decision that could make the difference between being thrown or keeping one's saddle.

Will trotted for a while then watched as Yeats and Harley cantered around the paddock. After a few minutes, Will asked to try cantering, so Yeats helped him do it. It was thrilling and he didn't fall. They took the horses back to their stalls, tethered them to the middle with lines on either side of their bridles, and groomed them. While cleaning the horses' hooves, Will commented on how some of the horses' shoes looked new. Yeats said his father had shoed the horses during his last visit. His father had put himself through university by working as a farrier and continued to shoe horses in Maine on a part-time basis, mostly during the summer when he didn't teach university classes.

Harley mentioned he should be aware of the back legs of a horse because, if spooked, its instinct was to kick, "And that won't be as much fun as it sounds." Yeats warned them against banging the stalls. To make his point, Yeats slammed the flat of his hand on a nearby stall and a rescue donkey called Tempest, standing in the last stall, leaned forward and gave his door a powerful kick that rattled the beams. Tempest didn't like loud banging.

Yeats drove a narrow truck into the barn and asked them to shift bags of manure from the truck to a dedicated area of the hayloft. This soupy manure in the plastic bags was sold to island gardeners.

Once Yeats was gone to his archery class, a bus pulled in with a group of participants who were met by their blue-shirted volunteers. Will tapped Harley on the shoulder and pointed to one of the volunteers who was coming over. It was Aubrey. Before he even made it to the front of the bus, Jason ran over, took him by the hand, and led him over to his mount in the paddock.

The therapeutic riders were out of sight when they heard a car pull into the parking lot, its tires scrunching over the loose gravel. Will and Harley continued hoisting manure bags three at a time on the big hook, then activated the electric hoist so it could be stacked at the back of the hayloft.

Will heard a car door open and close and glanced through the loft's air vent and froze. Bennett got out of the gray BMW driven by a redheaded woman. Will hissed to get Harley's attention, signaling for her to be quiet but to look in Bennett's direction.

Harley frowned, crossed over from where the manure bags were stacked, and stepped over some bales to peek through the vent. But by that time, Bennett had made his way to the opening to the stalls below.

"Hello, anybody home? Hello?" Bennett called out as he made his way past the truck and past Tempest's stall. He stopped there a moment and banged on the wall to get someone's attention. He got Tempest's attention. The rescue donkey kicked his stall door closed. Bennett jumped so high to the side, Will and Harley had to stifle a laugh.

"Can I help you?" said Yeats, who had just appeared behind the hay truck. "For their safety, we ask that visitors not enter the premises without being accompanied."

"Sorry, didn't know," said Bennett with a disarming smile. "I'm looking for Will McCoy and his cousin Harley McCann. I met Will downtown and he forgot his hat," said Bennett, holding up the powder-blue baseball cap with the Windy Farm horse logo on the front.

"I threw my hat as a decoy when they chased me," Will whispered to Harley as the two crouched and watched Yeats deal with Bennett.

"Are they volunteers here?" asked Yeats. "There are a lot of volunteers here who get to wear that hat. I'm afraid I don't know all of them. If you leave me the hat, I'll give it to my mother, Dr. Doan. She knows most of the — oh, there's mum now, why don't we talk to her? Who shall I say was looking for them? Hello? Hello?"

Will looked through the vent and saw Bennett hurry back to the gray BMW, which left in a shower of gravel as Dr. Doan looked on.

Will and Harley sidled over the big beams straddling the barn and dropped onto the bales of hay in the truck before swinging over the sides to the barn floor.

Harley answered Dr. Doan's puzzled look by saying, "That was the man Bennett, who hired us to sail *Wavelength* here and who made us dive for that wreck."

"Really?" said Dr. Doan, staring down the road the car had taken. "Well, that's not a good sign. The redheaded woman driving is Claire Calloway. She works for a man called Brian Ord. She manages the Ord Art Gallery for him in Hamilton."

As the therapeutic riders were coming back, Dr. Doan waved them inside her office, which was air-conditioned but also more private.

Dr. Doan sat in her big chair and waved her hand in a "sit down" gesture. Will and Harley did; Yeats leaned on the doorframe.

"Brian Ord is a very wealthy Bermudian. He inherited a fortune from his father and he made it grow. Not always in a legal or nice way, but he did make it grow. He's into art and real estate. Hector Ord, his father, launched the art thing. Hector was a good painter who some say made his money selling stolen works of art along with his forgeries. Like father like son."

Dr. Doan sighed and looked to her desk as she collected her thoughts. "I'm not sure how his son Brian Ord is involved with your wreck nor do I know why. But I can tell you that if Claire Calloway's involved with this man Bennett, it's with Brian Ord's knowledge. Now some Bermudians may not like to admit this, but the courts here will favor the island son over the tourist or expatriate, especially with his money and influence. You're going to need absolute proof of their guilt."

Will and Harley looked at each other.

"So what do we do?" asked Will.

"If you leave the island now, you might not be implicated

in the illegal wreck diving. But at the moment, you can't prove you were forced to do it, so if you do leave and the police tie you to the *Wavelength* and the wreck diving, you could be sent back here to face charges. Why don't you take some time to think your options through over lunch?" suggested Dr. Doan, rising to the sound of the lunch bell.

They trudged across the parking lot to the main building where volunteers were already carrying their lunch plates out to the tables under the veranda.

"What I don't understand," said Harley, "is why they're looking for us. They've found the wreck, right? So why are they still interested in us? And how are we to prove we're innocent in all of this?"

"We keep looking for *Wavelength*. That way we can prove the boat was used for illegal wreck diving and that we had nothing to do with it," was Will's quick reply. He didn't want to have to explain to Dr. Doan that Bennett wanted his letter back.

"It's a big island, full of marinas and places to moor a boat —" said Yeats before Will cut him off.

"St. George. I have a feeling we'll find something of interest in St. George."

Harley looked to Yeats for a comment. He shrugged. "As good as any place to look next."

Right after lunch, Yeats drove Will and Harley to the bus station in Hamilton. He had some business to take care of for the upcoming go-kart races that were scheduled for Sunday. Windy Farm was being paid to provide the bales of straw that would line the street and turns.

When they turned off the lane from Windy Farm to the road into town, Will spotted two guys sitting on their scooters smoking cigarettes. What caught his eye was the red fringe on the top of their black helmets. Just like the one Drury wore.

Chapter Twelve

St. George

*Minié bullet: Invented in 1849 by a French officer called
Minié, but Americans called it the "Minie" during its use
in the Civil War. Unlike the musket ball, it was conically shaped
and its bottom hollowed out. When gunpowder went off,
the gasses expanded the bullet's soft lead underbelly, snugging
it to the gun's barrel and harnessing more lethal force. Used with
the new spirals in the barrel, called rifling, it was lethal.*

As the bus sped toward St. George, Will pulled the old letter from
his backpack with care and handed it to Harley. "I told you I had
followed Bennett to the archives. Well, when he went out to take
a call, I grabbed this old letter he had."

"You took his letter?"

"Well, it wasn't to Bennett or from him. It was from a guy
called Papineau Benoit in St. George, Bermuda to his wife Lily in
Halifax and dated 1862. That's during the Civil War," he added,
without telling her that his dream about the shooting and the
fight on Penno's Wharf had made the time reference pretty clear.
"And this must be part of the letters they were talking about on
Wavelength, remember?"

"Okay, but why's he so interested in this letter if they've got the wreck?"

"I'm thinking that whatever they were looking for wasn't on the wreck. Bennett must think that this letter or the other letters will tell them where it is. Papineau Benoit — P.B., same letters that were on that box we found and I think that box is in this photo."

Will showed Harley the old card with Papineau's black and white photo on it as he leaned on a wooden box adorned with his initials. Will summarized the opening of the letter he had read where Papineau, recovering from the bullet that had broken his leg, had decided to resume command of his blockade-running boat:

> *With my leg still in a splint and still limping, I sailed the Almira to Charleston to deliver our cargo of rifled weapons and Minié bullets, which, ironically is the kind of weapon that was used to break my leg. This not the old musket and ball your father and I used to hunt moose.*

At the mention of the Minié bullet, Will produced the one he'd taken from Papineau's wooden box. He showed her the concave underbelly that flared out from the pressure of the exploding gunpowder and told her that with the new rifling in gun barrels the bullets were more effective. When she frowned, he explained how one could throw a conical football with a spiral farther and with more precision than a basketball or a soccer ball. Harley was athletic enough to understand. They read on.

> *During this trip, I insisted we also carry salt with us. The North has captured or destroyed salt works and without it the South can't butcher any cattle because the meat can't be preserved, and the leather can't be tanned for use in boots and belts for uniforms. I have seen families scrape salt from pickled meat, allow the brine*

to evaporate in the sun to harvest a few precious grains of salt. But what can they do, as time is against the South and they can't wait for the sun to do its work as they would normally do? Soldiers' limbs are amputated because, without salt to disinfect them, small cuts have become pestilent. There is little that is civil in this Civil War.

As the bus rounded a corner, they came into view of a cluster of boats moored in a cove. Harley scanned it with the binoculars Yeats had lent them. She shook her head. *Wavelength* was not in this cove. They turned their attention back to the letter.

> *While in Charleston I was shocked to see so many men with missing arms or legs, sometimes both, and frightened or dead eyes. They are in some ways victims of the war I feed with every cargo of weapons and munitions I bring over. Then I had a chance meeting with a barber, a free black called Joseph Rainey. I'd met the man six months ago in Bermuda when he was forced to work on a Confederate blockade runner. Despite being a free black man, he was coerced into digging fortifications around Charleston. He feared that things were about to get worse for him and his wife, Susan. I offered to take them to Bermuda.*
>
> *The night before we sailed from Charleston, I snuck them aboard. He passed as our long-serving steward while his wife, Susan, hid among the bales of cotton. When they proceeded to fumigate the bales and poke them through with a sharp rod to catch deserters, I produced Confederate agent John Tory Bourne's business card and told them they'd have to answer to him if we missed the tide — the best time to make a run through the blockade. They relented and we made off. I've done at least one honorable thing during this war.*
>
> *We unloaded the Raineys and our cotton in St. George and headed back to Wilmington with a load of uniforms, belts, and*

*boots as well as some of the new rifled cannons that spit death and
destruction with such precision.*

*We made it to Wilmington and awaited cotton bales to load
out. We make all this money while the good people of Wilmington
wither from want of basic food that we take for granted. These two
warring halves must find a way to be whole again.*

As Harley interrupted their reading to search a new bay with
the binoculars, Will watched two scooters pass them. The riders
glanced up at the passengers on the bus. Like Drury, both had
red tufts undulating from their black helmets. Will brought their
focus back to the letter by tapping it where they'd left off.

*We were informed that the owner had sold Almira to the
Confederate Navy. We felt abandoned. Then we hit the jackpot.*

*I booked return passage on a blockade runner to Bermuda.
We snuck past the blockaders on an outgoing tide, in the dead of
night and during a storm. We were well clear of the coast when we
saw two incoming ships tangle with the Union Navy. One boat was
struck by cannon fire. As she drifted in flames, her crew abandoned
her to scramble aboard the second boat and dash for the safety of
Wilmington.*

*As we passed the ship that was on fire, we figured she was
salvageable; the storm had already dampened the fire on her deck.
The Union Navy boats stopped firing upon her, probably because they
hoped to return and claim her as a prize after pursuing the second
fleeing boat.*

*The six senior crewmembers from the Almira and I decided
that we would instead claim her ourselves. The captain wouldn't
risk coming alongside. But he did sell us a longboat and slowed just
enough to let us launch her. We rowed to the stricken vessel, put the
fire out, and restarted one of the boilers before limping to Bermuda.*

She is a beauty, British built like so many of the newer generation of
blockade runners. British textile mills may be suffering from a lack
of cotton but their shipyards are working all out.

Our new vessel is 175 feet in length, has twin boilers, twin
Patch screws, telescoping funnels, and two masts that hinge back-
wards when needed to keep our silhouette off the horizon for as long
as possible, especially when approaching the American coast where
the North's navy watches for us. She's long, sleek, draws but 11 feet
fully loaded and vents steam underwater to allow her to run silent.

We have made the necessary repairs here in St. George and
await a load from the new Confederate agent Major Walker before
making once more for Wilmington. We have gone from hired crew
to shared ownership. And, my dear Lily, my partners have agreed to
rename her "H.M.S. Lily."

Captain. Peters' steward is clamoring for my letter so I must
close. With much affection to you and our son, from your faithful
husband, P.B.

Will looked up from the letter. "P.B. are the initials we found
on the box on the wreck. And Drury said it was 175 feet long. I
get the feeling that this blockade runner called *Lily* is the wreck we
were forced to dive on."

They got off the bus and walked toward the town square past
the beautiful St. Peter's Church, whose long rise of white steps
warned you that, beyond faith, you needed conviction and stamina
to come to this place of worship. Will bobbed around cars and
people, his eyes frantically darting.

"What are you so jumpy about, Will?" asked Harley with a
touch of annoyance.

"I'm looking for these guys I saw riding scooters. Their helmets
are the same as the one Drury was wearing the other day." But
Harley's dismissive headshake put an end to that explanation.

They still didn't know why Drury and Bennett hadn't found its precious cargo on the wreck and they didn't know where the other letters were and if they'd yield a clue.

They ambled down to the harbor, waited for the horse pulling a carriage with tourists to clip-clop past them, the white fringe of tassels on its canvas top undulating with the carriage's drowsy rocking motion. They crossed over to the Customs Building where they'd first landed to register *Wavelength*. This time, a big red tug with *Pilot* painted on its side was moored out front. From there they looked in both directions for *Wavelength* but saw nothing that even resembled her.

Will made a point of suggesting they go toward Penno's Wharf because he remembered that was where, in his dream, Papineau and Joseph had saved the man being beaten up by the Confederate sailors.

They had no more luck from that vantage point, so they walked back through the square toward St. Peter's Church. Will heard scooters revving their motors behind him and peeked over his shoulder just as the two riders with the red-crested black helmets came to a stop a block away.

Desperate to get off the street and not willing to let Harley's disbelief put them in jeopardy, Will grabbed her hand and yanked her inside the Bermuda National Trust Museum. Two towering chimneys painted white, while the rest of the building was a pale yellow, flanked the open wooden door.

"What are you doing, Will?" said Harley, shaking her wrist free.

"Hello and welcome to the Rogues and Runners Civil War Museum," said the woman behind the counter as she put down her e-reader.

"Uh, well, you know," stammered Will to Harley, "I just thought we'd check out the Civil War Museum to see if there's something here that confirms what we read in Papineau's letter." Will spoke in a low tone as he gestured to the Civil War memorabilia on the wall.

Will looked at paintings of paddle-wheel boats on the walls and asked, "Can you tell me, please, if one of your paintings shows the blockade runner called *Almira* or *Lily*?"

The woman behind the corner scrunched her eyes in thought before waving them over to the paintings in the far corner.

The canvas she was staring at captured a busy port scene with smaller crafts sailing between a number of steam-powered boats at anchor. Three of them were paddle wheelers; the fourth had the twin funnels of the screw steamer.

"That one," she said, pointing to the far paddle wheeler, "is *Almira*, while this one here is *Lily*. This watercolor was painted by Edward James. This is him here," she said, pointing to a figure in the corner of the painting. It was an image of a bearded, frail man with a straw hat, painting at an easel on the wharf — the painter Will had seen in his dream of the fight with Villiers Rougemont.

"He liked to paint himself into his portraits," said the guide with a smile that implied that she enjoyed James's sense of humor.

"Did he share a residence with a Mr. Allen?" asked Will, remembering that, in his dream, James had said to Mr. Allen that he'd "put the kettle on" when they got back home.

"Oh, you know, I think he did for a time, what with accommodations being so in demand here during the war. I do know that Mr. Allen hired him to paint the blockade runners and sent the paintings to the US Navy so they could intercept them when they ran to Wilmington or some other southern port. Mr. Allen was an enterprising man. He would make a second copy and sell that painting to the blockade runner's captain."

Will produced the card with Papineau Benoit's faded, black and white photo. "Can you tell me if this was the *Almira*'s captain?" he asked, hoping to confirm his findings.

"Oh, you have a *carte de visite*," said the woman, peering at it.

"A what?" asked Harley.

"A *carte de visite*, a calling card. They were quite the rage during the Civil War. All of these men with money in their pockets were able to afford them. As to your question, I don't have any record of who the *Almira's* captains were. I say captains, because boats often had different captains as they retired, were let go, or their boats were sold to different owners who might favor a different captain."

"Tell me," said Will as the woman returned to her position behind the counter, "was there a barber here, called Joseph, during the Civil War?"

"You're referring to Joseph Hayne Rainey," she answered.

"Did he shave and cut hair nearby?" Will asked.

"Yes, at the Tucker House, just over there." She flicked an index finger over her shoulder. "Unfortunately, it's closed today."

"Really?" asked Will with genuine disappointment. "That's a real shame. We're doing some research on his time here in Bermuda, after he escaped North Carolina."

On the wall, Will saw a black and white photograph of the man Papineau and Joseph Rainey had rescued in his dream. The caption said he was US Consul Charles Maxwell Allen.

"Mr. Rainey cut Consul Allen's hair, didn't he? That's what our research revealed. That, uh, that is, uh, correct, isn't it?" Will asked, fishing for more information. "And I believe Mr. Rainey helped save Consul Allen from a beating from some Confederate sailors, is that not right?"

"Oh, well, I don't know. It appears your research is a little more detailed than my knowledge. Confederate sailors here attacked him — Consul Allen, I mean — on a couple of occasions. That much we do know."

"And I believe his flagpole was cut down. That was on Penno's Wharf, right?"

"Well," she answered, a bit flustered at Will's knowledge,

"nobody's quite sure where Consul Allen had his office, but, yes, it's believed it was on Penno's Wharf. And yes, they did cut down his flagpole. What kind of research are you two doing? You seem quite young to be —"

"It's for my cousin Harley, here. She's going into journalism at Dalhousie University."

"Really?" said the woman, smiling.

"Oh, yes, I am going into journalism. And I love history and thought, you know, a little field research might help, with, uh —"

"Her admission essay," said Will, helping Harley out of a jam and ignoring the furious look she was giving him.

"Well," began the woman, "my niece is in second year there at Dalhousie University, studying law. I'll tell you what. It's quiet right now, so why don't I put the "back in five minutes" note on the door and let you have a peek inside Tucker House? It's so nice to see young people taking an interest in Bermudian history," said the woman, picking up a set of keys and leading them out.

"How much money would they make? Blockade runners, I mean," asked Will, curious if that was what Bennett was looking for on the wreck of *Lily*.

"Oh, well, every crew member had a different pay grade. The captain could usually earn five thousand dollars a trip. The next best paid was the pilot because if captured, he would not be exchanged or allowed to go free if he was American. The pilot's knowledge of, say the Cape Fear River made him too important to be released."

"And there were a lot of blockade runners doing this?" asked Harley as the woman locked the door behind them.

"Oh yes, indeed. You see, the South was the fourth largest economy in the world at that time. She had cotton, a commodity everyone wanted. They were surprised the Brits didn't side with them after hostilities started so they settled for running ships in with everything they needed. Most insisted on being paid in gold."

"So a ship that sank before it got to port might be loaded with the gold payment for the crew?" asked Will, giving Harley a knowing look.

"Yes, I suppose so," said the guide.

They walked around the corner, past a plaque that read, *Barber's Alley*.

The woman nodded to the sign, saying, "This was named in honor of Joseph Rainey." She unlocked the door, punched in the alarm code, and led them down to the right in what looked like the house's kitchen.

Coming down the stairs they passed a photo of Joseph Rainey with the same bushy sideburns Will had seen in his dream.

"Um," began Will, "he, Mr. Rainey, took reading and writing lessons here, didn't he?" Will asked, remembering the notebook full of corrections that had lain on the table. He ignored Harley's look questioning how he knew this.

"Well, yes, yes, he did. He was a free black man from the Carolinas, but in the South, it was illegal to teach blacks to read or write. Mr. Rainey saw an opportunity here and seized it. Bermuda, like all British colonies, had abolished slavery on August 1, 1834. After the war, he returned to North Carolina and was eventually the first black man elected to the US Congress, his seat being in South Carolina," said the woman, clasping her hands in front of her.

Will could feel Harley's stare burning into his back. He looked around the room for something to deflect her intensity and walked over to the sooty fireplace that was set up with rusty old pots instead of the clay pot he'd seen in his dream. But the comfortable-looking spindle chair with armrest that Papineau had sat in was right by the fireplace, and beside it was the very stool he'd rested his feet on while having a shave. Could the barber's money box still be in its hiding place he wondered?

Will pointed to the photo on the wall. "Is that Mr. Rainey?"

As the guide turned to the photo and nodded, Will leaned into the fireplace, reached up, and retrieved the little money box. He pried it open and couldn't believe his eyes; the folded letter was still there. He slipped it into his pocket and spun around.

"Oh dear, what's that?" asked the woman as Will handed her the tin box.

"I believe this is where Mr. Rainey kept his money," said Will, shaking the box, which rattled. He made a show of prying the lid open and dropped a tarnished coin in the bewildered woman's hand.

"Thank you so much for your help. We really do appreciate it. I think our five minutes are up," said Will with his most endearing smile as the woman stared wide-eyed at the coin and box in her hands.

Chapter Thirteen

Lily's Lament

Carte-de-visite: French for calling card, one with a black and white photo of the bearer, quite popular in the mid-1800s.

"What was that letter I saw you steal from that metal box?" whispered Harley in a reproachful tone.

"I didn't steal it. I, uh, I borrowed it. It looks like the one Papineau sent to his wife, that's why I took it," said Will, not wanting to tell her he'd seen it in his dream. "We can give it back to the Heritage Society before we leave, along with that gold necklace we found on the wreck. But after we figure out what Bennett and Drury were after, okay?" Harley nodded.

The cousins hurried into the White Horse pub, a white building whose dark green trim drew the eye to the veranda's cooling shade where they sat, overlooking the harbor. They had twenty minutes to kill before the next bus to Hamilton. Will was so excited his hands shook as he carefully unfolded the letter he'd taken from Rainey's money box.

This one was from Lily Benoit in Halifax to her husband, Papineau, in St. George, and dated July, 1863.

My dearest husband,

As soon as I got the baby to bed, I read and reread with great interest all of your news.

It is hard to read how your conscience is so aggrieved by your small part in supporting the slave-owning South. You speak of the great privations of the people of Wilmington. Perhaps, as captain and part owner of your ship, you can determine your cargo; eschew weapons and munitions for much needed food and such?

On another point, Alexander Keith Jr. has left Keith Hall where his uncle, brewmaster Alexander Keith, runs his empire. He opened his office on Hollis Street with that other Chebucto Grey (the all-white militia) blowhard, Benjamin Weir. They are falling all over themselves to be the agent of choice for all Confederates passing through. I have watched these smoking-room warriors disparage our noble Victoria Rifles militia unit simply because they are made up of blacks from Africville. We have nothing for which to reproach the south when it comes to hating the Negro.

Keith has taken rooms here at the hotel and once he starts to drink, pays me no heed and throws caution to the wind. I have heard him and Weir talk of the one million dollars Jefferson Davis has earmarked to pay for enterprising, behind-the-scenes acts of terror to be visited upon the North by whatever means available and regardless of loss of innocent lives, all to undermine the Union's will to fight. They seem to think that the Union's superior resources justify their cowardly choices of attacking civilian rather than military targets.

They hurried through her accounts of how Keith Jr. and his partner charged first-class rates for products they knew were inferior.

They float their mendacity upon a river of the best French champagne. I have heard him mention that he is looking to lease space on ships here and in Bermuda. My heart stilled when the name of your ship crossed their lips. I beg you, be very cautious in any undertaking with these men. Remember Keith is still rumored to be the man behind the 1857 explosion that leveled Halifax's gunpowder facility. Only his links to his famous uncle the brewer keep the authorities at bay.

I've shared my concerns with our hotel manager, who upbraided me for even listening in on the conversations, while I could do no less without blocking my ears. He says we are not here to judge our guests but to cater to their needs. Money. It is always about money. And being that we are in need of my income and yours to clear our family debts, I too keep quiet in order to keep my wages.

The manager took advantage of the situation to insist that I change my last name to give it an English tone. He said it gave the hotel guests a sense of comfort to know they were being cared for by their own kind. He pointed out that I was the last to do so, that Marie Maisonneuve is now known as Mary Newhouse, that Phillipe Gervais, our doorman, has become Phil Jarvis. So now I have gone from Lily Benoit to Mrs. Lillian Bennett. Know, my dear Papineau, that I do this with great reluctance and not without a certain degree of shame. When you return in a more permanent fashion, I will gladly again take on your good Acadian name.

With all the affection time and distance allows me to express, your Lily.

Will looked up from the letter out to the harbor where the wind herded the waves in a steady convoy of white caps, pushing the reality that was dawning on them both.

Harley dialed the older cellphone Dr. Doan had lent them.

"Dr. Doan, it's Harley. Could you check with that person you know, the one who told you nobody by the name of Phillip Bennett had recently landed in Bermuda, and check instead if someone called Phillip Benoit has? ... Yes, with an 'o,' 'i,' 't' at the end. Thank you," she finished, clicking it off.

Will said out loud the conclusion they'd both come to, "Bennett. He's Papineau Benoit's descendant, isn't he? That's why he knows about these letters."

"And I wonder," said Harley, "if his wife was right in fearing that those men might hire Papineau. Did they have anything to do with the shipwreck?"

The cellphone rang.

"This is Harley ... Yes, thank you Dr. Doan. That does make sense now ... Well, I'll explain what little we know as soon as we get back ... Yes, we're catching the next bus to Hamilton ... Okay, that's nice of Yeats. Thanks," said Harley, getting up as she finished her conversation.

She nodded to Will, "Bennett is Benoit, which puzzles me because he showed his driver's license with the name Bennett to me when he ordered those new sails in Lunenburg. Now that I think of it, Grandpa thought it was a bit strange that he paid for the new sails with cash. Probably so we couldn't trace a check or a credit card transaction. C'mon, let's get the bus. Yeats will pick us up in Hamilton."

As long as Bennett, Drury, Claire Calloway, or the scooter riders with red-tailed black helmets don't get them first, thought Will. Their list of enemies was growing.

Chapter Fourteen

The Admiralty House

*Pintail: A piece of iron jutting from wood or stone at a 90 degree
angle to hang a rudder or a hinged gate or door.*

Will helped Sherman to haul the fish he was giving to Windy Farm
upstairs. "Fresh caught this morning," is how he qualified it.

"Your accent," began Will, "doesn't sound like —"

"I'm from Bermuda? I know. See, when I was six, my daddy
got a job as a diesel mechanic in South Carolina. We lived there
till I was sixteen. When he moved us back here and became a
fisherman, I worked with him. That accent and an attitude's about
all I brought back with me."

"Oh. Well, I wondered why you didn't sound like Aubrey,"
said Will.

"How's Aubrey fitting in here now? I gather he's spending most
mornings here, that right?"

"He's helping with that boy Jason. Right, Humbert?" Will
asked the parrot as he lugged a milk crate full of fish filets in plastic
bags.

"You betcha," squawked Humbert from his perch in the cage,
a feathered soldier doing an emphatic two-step.

"You been friends long? With Aubrey, I mean. You seem to care 'bout him a lot. Especially the other day, you know, when he was sitting out in the ocean with his suit on," Will asked.

"Him leaving us would be a waste of a good heart," grunted Sherman.

They stopped to catch their breath. Sherman sleeve-wiped perspiration from his brow, which left a dark crescent in the faded green shirt where his arm crooked.

"How'd you come to know Aubrey?"

Sherman opened the freezer and removed the contents from one side. He answered Will's questioning look by saying, "Gonna put this fresh stuff on the bottom, then pile this older fish on top so's they eat the previously frozen food first."

Will helped him stack the frozen packages on the table beside Humbert.

"Must be going on twenty-five, no, more like thirty years ago, I met Aubrey. Man was doing good for hisself. He had quit school at fourteen to work as a stonecutter with his father full time. Then he bought that quarry that's across the road, behind his house. He done so well for hisself, he bought that piece of land his house is on now and commenced to build hisself a new house."

The mist rising from the frozen food on the table as it contacted the warm Bermudian breeze swirled a steam bath of cool air around Humbert, who two-stepped his contentment.

"Now you got to understand, that back then, no black person had ever lived in that parish. Aubrey was the first. So on that first day he built the walls of what would become the kitchen, parlor, and bedroom. You'll notice if you look that he's since added to it, made it bigger when he married and had his son."

"That would be Anthony?" queried Will.

"That would. Now Aubrey's a big man. Was bigger and faster back then. He'd cut limestone block and had it all figured out. He had a horse and cart that carried all them blocks across the road. Unfortunately, understanding and tolerance didn't greet him when he crossed that road. No sir, no sir."

Sherman placed the last bag of fish from his crate into the bottom of the freezer, then signaled for Will to start loading his.

"Aubrey was a wonder to watch. He had loaded his cart the night before, so he and his horse arrived on his new property when it was dark and early. He started mixing mortar by coal light and when the sun got its lazy self outta bed, Aubrey had laid out and positioned the whole perimeter of his house. By night-fall, them walls were up and held together by mortar, blood and sweat. That evening, he went back to the small cottage he lived in, back a' the quarry, and he must'a slept the sleep of the righ-teous that evening. But it wasn't the righteous who came calling that night, no sir, no sir," said Sherman, looking out the window toward the covered paddock as he recollected the moment with a tremor in his voice.

He shook his head for emphasis, or perhaps out of sadness for the memory. "He came back in the next morning's darkness to see that his walls 'ad all been pushed over 'fore the mortar could do its work and bind things," he said, holding his fists firm like the mortar was supposed to have done.

"Pushed over?" Will asked as he closed the freezer top and followed Sherman back downstairs. Sherman nodded.

"See," started Sherman as he thumped down the stairs, "neigh-bors wanted him to understand that they wasn't going to sit idly by and let a black man move into the neighborhood. Wasn't the kind o' change they was prepared to accept."

"What did he do when he saw his walls thrown to the ground like that?"

Sherman stopped in the shade of the veranda and a little smile crept to the corners of his mouth as the memory of the moment took center stage.

"He hummed. Yes, sir, he hummed. A hymn. Then he began to collect all his fallen stone and, with his mason's hammer, knocked off the useless mortar that hadn't worked for him, no how. He started to rebuild. And he sang. He sang that whole day long with a voice that would still an angel in mid-flight."

"You saw this?" asked Will to be sure the story was accurate.

"Yes sir, I did. I watched him for about an hour. Then I started singing with him and lifting blocks from where they'd landed. 'Bout that time, my wife brought me some coffee in a thermos. She couldn't believe what she saw." A big belly laugh interrupted Sherman's narration.

"There I was helping the man sort out his blocks. Told my wife I wouldn't be going fishin' that morning and to call my father to tell him so. I spent the day rebuilding the walls that small-thinking people had knocked down. We spent the night sittin' by a fire in the clearing by the house, making sure the mortar had a fighting chance this time. Oh, they came again to do their wicked work. We saw their shadows appear on the edge of the clearing, then rustle back into the darkness from whence they came," finished Sherman with a nod to the positive ending to his recollection.

"Wow. So that's how you became friends?"

"Started thataway," said Sherman, shuffling back to his van.

"I told him that I couldn't go to church with the same parishioners who thought that going to church on Sunday and knocking a man's house down on Friday because of the color of his skin was the Christian thing to do. So Aubrey, bless his soul, he invites me to go to *his* church."

"Well, that was nice of him," said Will.

Sherman stopped by his van. "You don't understand there, Will. His church, well, his church back then hadn't had a white parishioner, ever. So there I was on a Sunday morning, walking up to the Reverend Boswell, who was outside greeting his parishioners. The line's shrinking and I'm gettin' up to him. Aubrey had said he'd be there but he was nowhere in sight and it was a few minutes before service and I wondered if he was maybe waiting for me in the shade of the vestry so I stayed in line. Everyone stopped to look. Those who'd gone in? They all stopped just inside the door to see how the reverend was going to deal with it. With me," said Sherman, leaning on his van, savoring the memory.

"Don't mind telling you I was in a sweat. And not just 'cause of the weather, no sir, no sir. So it's finally my turn and I says, 'Good morning, Reverend.' 'How can I help you?' he answers, narrowing his eyes and clutchin' his Bible. 'Well,' says I, 'I was hopin' you wouldn't mind me joining your congregation.' The reverend pressed his lips together, 'cause he was understandably steamed about me standing there with a preposterous notion. 'I will not stand idly by while you blaspheme in front of our church,' he blustered. I thought I'd faint dead away when a big hand clapped my shoulder from behind and Aubrey says, 'Morning Reverend. This is Sherman. I found the tenor the choir's been looking for.' The Reverend looked like he'd been hit by one of Aubrey's blocks thrown from a distance and at a great pace."

Sherman opened the door to his van to let it cool down. "I've sung with the choir ever since. I was the poorest voice among those boys but in my little way, I was also the richest soul. The irony was that the Reverend's sermon that day, because he'd heard what had happened to Aubrey's walls, was about tolerance. So he preached tolerance as my frightened white face looked out from the front row of the choir."

"And the neighborhood finally accepted him?" asked Will, eager for a happy ending.

"Took a full while, it did. 'Course, him being Bermuda's best cricketer helped build tolerance. Still took a while to climb over that wall. Heck, took almost a year 'fore my wife agreed to join me in church."

"So what happened the other day? I mean, why was he sitting there, just, you know, just waiting for a big wave to ...," asked Will, not quite able to finish his question.

"Always hard to predict what will topple an empire," answered Sherman. "But don't you be thinking of Mr. Aubrey Dill as some sort of Bermuda shipwreck now, hear? Man's not done by a long shot. Like I said, losing Aubrey would be a waste of a good heart."

Sherman backed his van away from the building and stopped long enough to lean out of the window and say, "I keep looking for that boat of yours, *Wavelength*. They may be moving it around and could end up taking it to a harbor or cove you've already looked at." With a wave of his hand that was more of a waggle, he was off.

Will stood there thinking that yes, they should still be looking for *Wavelength* to prove their innocence. But they did have certain responsibilities to Windy Farm, if only to compensate for room and board.

Will looked up as Yeats eased his scooter off the center stand and started the motor.

"Where you off to, Yeats?" he called, striving to keep his voice friendly.

"Hamilton. Off to make final calculations on how many bales of straw we'll need for the go-kart race. It's a big deal for us here on the island. And for the farm. They rent the bales to use as a safety buffer along the route. We get 'em all back plus an installation and removal fee. Big help with all this," he said, twirling a finger around to encompass the farm, then added, "You know there'll be cameras from all over the world watching this race?"

"Can I come with you? You know, to have a look in the harbor, in case *Wavelength* has come into port."

Yeats nodded, put the bike on the side stand, opened the big black carry box on the back, handed Will a helmet and waved him aboard.

It wasn't a big motor. Most Bermuda scooters weren't big. This one, Yeats explained, had a 125 cc engine. The island only allowed bikes to go up to 150 cc. However, it was plenty fast enough to scare Will.

They pulled into the car park opposite a restaurant and bar called The Pickled Onion. Yeats excused himself and scooted over to the sidewalk to shake hands with a man in yellow Bermuda shorts with a pale blue shirt and matching tie.

Will took advantage of the break to scan the harbor with the small binoculars he'd brought. He lingered here and there when a sailboat hidden by another boat might just be *Wavelength*. But one by one, none proved to be the fugitive boat.

Will leaned back on the seaside railing and scanned the stores near the doorway Drury had used the night Will had spotted him while sailing with Sherman. Will raised the binoculars and froze.

On the top floor balcony was Brian Ord, the man he'd seen in the boat that had come close to *Wavelength* and who had given Bennett the order to "make it look like an accident."

He had on the same hat with the floppy, broad brim, the gauze covering his face and hands, and the same oversized sunglasses. His hands were lying in his lap. He sat in his wheelchair taking in what must have been a breathtaking view. The door behind him swung open and out came Claire Calloway, her red mane flying in a sudden onshore gust.

She put her hand on Ord's shoulder before moving to the railing and looking out. Her gaze drifted till it rested on Will, who was looking up with his binoculars. She dialed her cell and turned her head inward to talk before straightening out to point directly at Will. She hammered the air, which Will understood to mean that whatever she wanted to have happen, it had to be now and it had to be to him. Not a good idea to linger longer.

Yeats ambled back over as he finished committing figures to his phone, closing it and tucking it into his pocket.

"Hey, Yeats, I think we should really move from here right now. That woman Calloway, she's up there on the balcony — no don't look back. Let's just get out of here fast, okay? She was giving someone orders and I'm sure it wasn't to get our autographs."

Yeats sprang the two helmets from the carrier, revved up the engine and slipped into traffic. Will risked a glance by the door to the building where he saw three red-feathered black helmets on parked scooters, their owners sprinting for their bikes as he and Yeats roared past. Well, as much of a roar as a 125cc scooter can muster.

Out of the corner of his eye he saw Calloway wheel Ord back into his penthouse. Yeats shot down the road, past the "birdcage," then past the Hamilton Princess Hotel, when Will said, "This isn't the way back to Windy Farm, is it?"

"Nope. But I'm not leading those jerks in the Red Feather Gang back to the farm."

"The guys with those red tufts on their helmets?" asked Will.

Yeats nodded, then wove his scooter in and out of traffic with a frightening surge of adrenaline. As Will glanced over his shoulder, one thing was certain: the three gang members weren't gaining.

They sped along Pitts Bay Road then St. John's Road till they turned into a parking lot leading to Admiralty House. Yeats sure could handle a scooter.

He braked, waved Will off the back seat, backed it in to a parking spot, and pulled it up on the center stand. He opened the storage box, slid their two helmets inside, insisting that they toss their shirts, shoes, socks, watches, phones and wallets in there as well. Then he motioned for Will to follow.

For a reason Will couldn't understand, Yeats stopped in full view of the three members of the gang, who pulled their scooters into the same parking lot.

"What did you call those guys?" asked Will as Yeats resumed his steady pace away from their pursuers.

"The Red Feather Gang," answered Yeats. "These guys are a bunch of unemployed youths who have been involved in small-time robberies. Their leader's a guy called Dwayne something or other. He's in Westgate Prison with charges pending. But I don't fancy tangling with them so we're going to lead them on a wild-goose chase," answered Yeats, scrambling along a dock with a concrete bench carved into the shore-side rock. They passed a rusty cannon sunk perpendicularly into the rock, possibly as a bollard to hold ships fast, continuing along a beautiful swimming cove before slowly climbing some stairs, apparently wanting their pursuers to see where they were heading.

They skipped down stairs carved into the rock, brushing past broad plant leaves that tried to hide the damage to the land that had been caused by the military tunneling. There were rusty pintails on the left side where once had hung a door.

They passed a rectangular opening cut into the cave wall that allowed a glimpse of Bermuda's opal waters.

"The Brits had a gun battery here once," shot Yeats as he plunged farther into the cavern. It was a good thing that Yeats knew his way because it was dark. Will followed Yeats's example and ran his right hand along the wall as a guide and kept his left in front of him so he could tap Yeats's back to avoid slamming into him. He winced once or twice as his bare feet clipped the top of a sharp point of stone.

Eventually the tunnel widened into a room whose floor opened two yards above the sea that washed in under an over-hang. The pool of emerald water was surrounded by walls of sharp, nasty-looking rock from which reflections played like water running down the walls' striated surfaces. Curt voices closed in behind them.

"Okay," whispered Yeats, "follow my lead and we'll swim back around to the steps we passed and go back to the parking lot. Be sure to jump out far enough to land in the middle."

Before Will could ask him if he was crazy, Yeats leaped away from the rocky outcropping, landed with a small splash, surfaced, swam out of Will's way and waved for him to follow. The voices of their pursuers erased Will's doubts.

He leaped, waving his arms like a flightless bird. Whoosh, he hit and went under. Before he surfaced in the marvelously warm water, he felt Yeats tugging at him to swim out of the cave and into the open sea. Will spat out the salty water and wiped his hair back from his eyes. The sight of the open sea that stretched before them startled him. Rougher seas would have battered them against the rock.

Yeats did the Australian crawl along the shore. And he did it with great precision, not with that inefficient side-to-side head-sway of those who couldn't do it properly. Did Robin Hood have to do everything so well?

They swam into the cove and climbed the stairs in a crouch. Yeats put his finger to his lips then sprinted back to the scooter past a bewildered mother pushing her child in a stroller.

They slid on their street clothes and helmets before Yeats eased them back into traffic, making their way back to the safety of Windy Farm.

Chapter Fifteen

Spreading Manure

*Compound bow: a bow that uses pulleys to harness
power more effectively than a long bow.*

With the use of a calling card to avoid expensive long-distance
fees, Harley called her grandfather and told him a lot of half-
truths: the ride had been exciting, and yes, they had managed to
get some scuba diving in, apparently on a Civil War-era wreck.
When he laughed and asked if they'd uncovered any lost treasure,
she winced and said not yet.

Then Will called his mother in Toronto and spoke to her and
his grandparents, telling them he and Harley were having an
amazing adventure, which was true, that they loved the people
and horses at Windy Farm, which was true, and that they were just
helping out around the farm before they flew home, which was
mostly true.

The cellphone was quite old but it did have a voice recorder, so
he asked Humbert, "So, did that sound good?"

He recorded him saying, "You betcha." He then played it back
to Humbert who tilted his head to the side in puzzlement.

Will laughed as he crossed the parking lot and came up behind
Aubrey, who was leaning on the railing to the covered paddock.

Jason climbed up two of the rungs so he could lean on the top railing beside Aubrey, their shoulders now almost at the same height.

It made an interesting picture, the tall, broad-shouldered black man in casual clothes with his right leg crossed behind his left one, while beside him a skinny white boy stood on the second rung mimicking one leg tucked behind the other.

Without looking at Aubrey, Jason said, "Dr. Doan says that I'm not well because of what I saw happen to my parents. Dr. Doan says she thinks I'll get better. But that could take a while, you see. That's how come I start to shake and make that sound when I get nervous. And I get nervous a lot, Mr. Aubrey. So, I've been thinking about what you said yesterday, about us being friends. Because I'm sick, maybe I'm not the best friend you could have right now."

Aubrey continued to stare into the dark paddock and made a little "hmmm" sound to indicate he was thinking. "Well, Jason, I think I'd prefer to be with you sick, than with anybody else who's well."

They stared into the darkness of the paddock where a horse could be heard pawing the earth like a drum, until Jason finally said, "Okay then, Mr. Aubrey."

Will strode over to where Dr. Doan was working the elevated vegetable bins. They were about hip-high for people in wheel chairs and with limited mobility who couldn't bend down to work a more traditional garden. These were rectangular containers running about ten feet in length, four feet in width and a foot deep, all sprouting green life.

"Can I ask you about Aubrey, Dr. Doan?" On her nod he asked, "What happened to his son, Anthony?" Will picked up a pair of gardening gloves that were sitting on a wheelbarrow and slipped them on.

With her eyes on her work, Dr. Doan explained, "Aubrey became a very successful businessman. The story goes that he determined he'd make a success of himself and earn the respect of others. He built up his quarry work and hired a team of men to work for him, cutting stone for roofs and walls and actually making the repairs or installations on houses all over Bermuda. His was a one-stop shop. Then he expanded into the water business, cleaning the roofs and cisterns, and then filling up the newly cleaned cistern. His is one of the biggest water companies on the island. But all that work meant he delayed other things — like marriage. So he married late and had a son they called Anthony. Aubrey's wife died a few years after the boy was born, and people say that Aubrey immersed himself in his work and took Anthony with him when he played cricket. Anthony eventually took over the water business but according to newspaper reports, unbeknownst to Aubrey, Anthony had taken to drinking, and worse, drinking when driving."

"Four months ago there was a terrible crash. Anthony had been out late with one of the company trucks. He went through a stop sign and killed a young man on a scooter — both dead. That was the first and only time Aubrey had any inkling that his son was something other than an upstanding citizen. When the police announced that his son was highly intoxicated at the time of his death, well it really took the wind out of Aubrey's sails. Often our children are our only conclusive proof that we have lived, and that proof is an essential aspect of being human."

Will took his lead from Dr. Doan who pulled up Bermuda onions and carefully worked the precious soil from the roots back into the bin before piling them in a bushel basket.

"When he saved our lives the other day, well, I think he was sitting on the boiler just hoping for a big wave to come along and take him away. He was dressed in his wedding suit. Said he was planning on meeting up with the spirit of his dead wife. He had closed up his house. Turned everything off — the water, gas, electricity, all of it. He wasn't planning on coming home, that's for sure," said Will in a soft, sad voice, staring at Dr. Doan, hoping she'd offer some hope for Aubrey's wellbeing.

"People say you have to move on from a disaster but in fact you don't. You have to find a way to carry on, to carry the pain with you. Because if you can't carry it, it crushes you."

Will held the prongs up and let them drip over the bin and said, "He seems to be getting on pretty good with that kid Jason, right?"

She nodded in a non-committal way, and said, "Sometimes, when a lost soul finds someone more vulnerable than themself, it awakens hope, becomes an antidote."

Will laid the pitchfork and the shovel across the wheelbarrow and rolled it beside Dr. Doan, who carried the bushel basket of onions back to Windy Farm's kitchen.

"Charles Darwin found that it's not the strong, or the clever ones who survive, Will. It's the ones who can adapt that survive." What she left unsaid was that she wasn't sure if Aubrey could adapt, or if he'd survive. Will's father hadn't survived, Aubrey's wife and son hadn't survived, and now Aubrey might not either.

Yeats drove the small truck across the parking area, into the barn. He and Harley had loaded it with bags of fresh manure to, once again, be stacked in the hayloft.

Dr. Doan continued on to the kitchen with her onions while Will wheeled the barrow to the side of the barn where he hosed the tools off before hanging them up in spots that were identified by their painted profiles.

Will nodded to one of the volunteers, who tied four saddled horses to the outside railing where Aubrey and Jason had stood before they returned to Hamilton. Yeats went into the office to do paperwork while Will joined Harley.

Barn swallows swooped around them and up to their nests above the rafters as Will helped Harley hook six plastic bags of manure at a time to the big industrial hook. It ran along a track in the shape of an H that spanned the length of the barn and could make a right or left turn at either end. An orange switch box linked to an electrical panel by a thick black cable coordinated the industrial hook's functions.

Will made the mistake of letting it swing back to its resting place, slamming it against the wall. Tempest the donkey responded by hoof-slamming his stall door closed. Will sheepishly made his way down the stalls to open it again. A loose mesh was secured on the outside to keep the animals in while letting air circulate.

Harley went up to the hayloft while Will loaded six bags on the hook, each bag weighing about ten kilos. On Will's command, the hydraulic lift hauled the load above the truck's cab, swaying all the way to the end of the barn, then to the right till he heard Harley yell, "Stop." He'd lower it till she'd again yell stop and he'd wait for her to unload before reversing the process and starting anew. While the naked hook ran back to him, Harley stacked the bags in an overlapping manner so the piles wouldn't topple.

After three loads, to avoid repetitive strain, Harley called down for them to switch places. Harley clambered over the bales of hay and clattered down the ladder where Will pulled a few strands of hay from her hair. She gave him a big smile and it felt like old times, when it was just the two of them. When Yeats wasn't in the picture. He really had to stop thinking like this.

They loaded six more bags onto the hook and he showed Harley how to hoist and move them down the track. Just as they were to send them to the right, five back-lit figures filled the open doorway at the back of the barn.

Their tufted scooter helmets marked the five men as members

of the Red Feather Gang. And the man with the gun in his hand
standing in front laughing, was Drury.

"So, Harley, Will. How are you guys? We've missed you," he
said with false good humor before his tone changed to nasty. "But
we mostly missed the letter you stole from us. We want it back
and you too. So step away from the truck and come over here,
won't you? Before I lose my cool."

From the corner of his eye, Will saw Yeats toe open the door
to his mother's office, pull the big compound bow's string back
with a wicked-looking arrow lying in wait, then ease into the
doorway.

"Down! Now!" hissed Yeats.

Will and Harley dropped to a crouch as Yeats stepped out of
the entranceway and let his arrow whistle over their heads. The
three-pronged tip pierced the tops of the six bags of manure. The
weakened plastic ripped open, drenching the gang with its brown,
soupy contents.

Drury leaped backward into the doorway to Tempest's stall.
He leaned forward and stuck his head out and laughed at the
plight of his gang members who stood, shoulders stooped, trying to
shake off the liquid manure that seeped into their white clothing.

Still leaning forward, Drury swung his gun around to point it
at Will, Harley, and Yeats. "Nice move. Now drop everything in
your hands and keep 'em in sight."

As a barn swallow swooped in and made Drury flinch, Will
swung the hydraulic control against the near wall. Clang!

Tempest double-hoofed the door to his stall. Almost ripped
from its hinges, the door whacked Drury in the butt, skidding
him face-first into the smelly, soupy mess on the floor.

Chapter Sixteen

The Banyan Tree

Bermuda Railway Trail: Eighteen miles of the old railway that
ran the length of Bermuda from 1931 to 1948 have had
the old tracks removed so it can be used as a walking
and bicycling trail, with occasional use by equestrians.

Two gang members laughed when the donkey's kick sprawled Drury into the pooling dung.

Drury sputtered, spat, and spewed, "My gun. Get my gun."

Yeats whirled Will around and pushed him through the barn door. Harley was a half-step ahead of him.

Yeats sprang Harley into the saddle of the first horse, then Will into the second, before he vaulted into the third.

He yanked the reins hard left and rose into the stirrups. His mount bent its head down to gain traction as it lunged in the direction of the path that ran outside the paddock and into the wooded lot. Will and Harley's mounts galloped in pursuit, their hooves throwing up clumps of red earth in their wake.

As the horses and riders thundered along the path, Will risked a look back over his shoulder. On the far side of the barn, the five members of the Red Feather Gang scrambled back to their scooters, some shaking their arms in a vain attempt to rid themselves of the coating of dark brown manure.

Thumping hooves and the haoh, haoh, haoh that grunted its way through his horse's lungs drowned out the scooters roaring to life.

Yeats led Will and Harley around the border of an adjacent farm. The gang members, their white jackets streaked in dark brown, skidded their scooters in pursuit.

A tractor straddled the edge of a field and the earthen path that they cantered along. Knee-high red stumps studded the ground, which, as Will got closer, turned out to be bags of plastic webbing full of potatoes. Two field hands pulled up spuds, dropping them into a bushel basket before tumbling them into the red bags awaiting retrieval. The two pickers gawked as the three mounts thundered through, their riders standing in their stirrups like race jockeys.

Yeats veered to kick over a full bag, bouncing potatoes along the path. A picker yelled. It was nothing compared to the cursing and yelling from the gang as potatoes twisted their scooters' small wheels, sprawling half of them into the field's red earth.

A long, mounded rectangle of stone and earth marked the end of one farm and the beginning of another. With only enough room for one horse, Yeats reined in his mount as they traversed farms, from a field of lettuce to a field of corn where the sound of hooves echoing off stone walls startled three of the feral chickens that roamed freely through Bermuda.

At the end of the second farm, Yeats swung his horse onto a narrow path that led them to a long, broader trail. In places it was on flat ground, while in others, it had been carved into the rock and Will wondered where they were and why there were no cars, even if the narrow path could only have accommodated one car at a time.

They slowed at a padlocked metal gate. There was a shin-high stile that allowed pedestrians and horses to cross.

They reined in at the first road that intersected their route. Will read a sign: "No motorized vehicles." Another told him that they were riding on "The Bermuda Railway Trail," built in the 1930s.

Yeats took advantage of a slowdown in car traffic to spur his horse forward by squeezing his heels into the ribs and clicking his tongue, just like Aubrey had done when he'd led Jason's horse on that first walk.

There was a yell from behind. Will saw a man and a woman on the far side of the stile being jostled sideways as the Red Feather Gang roared down the Railway Trail two abreast.

While the gang members four-handed each scooter over the stile, Yeats led the horses further along the path. Here the trumpet-like flowers on the tall hibiscus bushes blared their passage in hues of blue, white and pink.

At a turn in the trail, a feral chicken leaping from a chest-high perch spooked Will's mount. It shot sideways, the momentum flinging Will from the saddle, his hands unable to cling to the mane. He slid along the horse's flank, spooking it even more.

Will grabbed one of the big curving branches lining the trail but it bowed under his weight. He landed on a clump of thick-leaved plants, which broke his fall instead of a rib. He rolled tight to the foliage to avoid Harley's horse.

Yeats spun his horse around just as Will's mount cantered past him. He circled back beside Will, slipped his left foot out of the stirrup and reached down. "C'mon, Will. Get up and get on."

Harley reined her horse around as she pointed behind them. "They're coming. You've got to move now, Will."

The fall had knocked the wind out of Will. But the sight of the first scooter coming around the bend got him to his knees, then to his feet. He grabbed Yeats's outstretched left hand and with his right, gripped the far side of his saddle. Yeats leaned way over, springing Will up till he could slip his left foot into the empty stirrup and swing his right leg over the horse's rump.

Yeats took his stirrup back, saying, "Hang on there, Will." For the second time in as many days, Will found himself gratefully wrapping both arms around Yeats as danger closed in on them. For a moment, Will wondered if this is what having a big brother would be like.

They rode into a tunnel and emerged at the far side to more stone walls where banyan tree roots tentacled up the vertical surfaces to the sun that hardly reached the railway floor.

Yeats pulled up. "Okay," he said, catching his breath. "We can't outrun them with two of us on a horse. So climb these roots to the top. Then go left along this road till you come to the next one. Sherman's got his fish stand up there on the right and he'll help you get to Aubrey's place. Best if you're not around Windy Farm right now. For you and the participants."

"Can't we go to the police now that Drury's come to the farm and waved that gun around?" Will asked, sliding to the ground and patting Yeats's horse above the white foam lathering its neck from the exertion in the heat. It wasn't good for the horses to continue at a pace that scooters could maintain forever.

Yeats shook his head. "If we call the police, the gang will say they came to ask about riding horses or something. It'll be our word against theirs. That guy Drury won't be carrying a weapon when they arrest him. Then you're back to proving you had nothing to do with smuggling gear aboard a boat that you still can't find. And if you mention Brian Ord's name, well then you're really up against it because he won't take lightly to being accused of kidnapping and plundering wrecks."

Yeats's horse nodded his head as if the truth of his statement was too obvious for a whinny. The rock face echoed the collective rumble of scooters closing in. Yeats flicked his chin upward to hurry them.

Harley edged her horse closer to the webbing of big gray roots. She handed Yeats her reins and put her right foot into a gap in the overlapping vegetation, finding toe and hand holds as she went.

Will waited till she was at the top of the fifteen-foot climb before following suit.

Yeats waited and watched. "What about my horse?" asked Will before stepping off the banyan tree to grip the stone wall like Harley was doing.

"She'll be fine. I'll catch her up and take them home through some paths those scooters can't follow." And with a click of his tongue their horses trotted off down the path.

Will and Harley slipped over the stone fence and walked in the direction Yeats had directed them to go. They stopped to watch Yeats spur the horses up a three-foot rise in the wall and disappear into a thicket.

They dropped to a crouch and peeked through a crack in the wall as the Red Feather Gang pulled up and stared in the direction Yeats had disappeared.

"Where the hell are the other two?" bellowed Drury as he raced his scooter up and down the path, peering into the foliage to find them. "Oh hell, Claire's gonna be some steamed —" He looked up and saw Will and Harley, who ducked down too late.

"They've climbed to the road above. Let's get 'em," screamed Drury.

Chapter Seventeen

The Fish that Got Away

*Old man's beard: Pale green lichen that grows in trees
in various parts of the world and looks like a beard.*

Will and Harley hurried on to the next road where Sherman had a
big tent extending from his van onto the sidewalk. Sherman had
six big coolers out and a number of people had stopped to buy
fish from him.

Sherman's smile when he saw them faded as he took in Will's
bruised face, torn shirt, and the trickle of blood where he'd
strained one of Aubrey's stitches in his fall. He picked up on their
nervousness as they kept checking over their shoulder. He signaled
for Will and Harley to duck through the van's sliding door. The
cousins slumped to the floor of the vehicle and caught their
breath, so grateful for the safety of the van that they weren't bothered by the odor. They might have smelled like a fish but they'd be
the ones that got away.

Sherman had almost sold his whole catch. He passed them a big
bottle of water and finished up with two customers.

After a brief explanation from the cousins, Sherman packed
up and drove them to Aubrey's house. On the way, Will fell asleep
with his head on Harley's shoulder. The chase, the ride, the fall,

and the eventual escape had exhausted him and his eyelids closed on their own.

They pulled into Aubrey's place and this time it didn't look like the house was getting ready to be shut down. As soon as they stepped out, Harley flattened him and herself against the side of Sherman's truck, forcing Will to crouch with her. She put her finger to her lips, then made a twisting motion with her hand, like one would twist the throttle on a scooter. Sure enough, as the rattle of Sherman's diesel motor ebbed, Will could hear the putt-putt of an idling scooter.

Will followed Harley in behind a breeze block wall. Peering through one of the openings, they saw a rider with a red-feathered helmet slowly come into view. When Sherman strode around to look at him, the rider took off.

"You think he saw us?" asked Will.

Sherman's double beep on the horn brought Aubrey, wearing a knee-length apron and wiping his hands on a tea towel, out from the kitchen. He tossed it over a shoulder as Hamlet scooted out from behind him and gave Will and Harley a vigorous tail-shaking welcome.

Sherman insisted they take a big red snapper for dinner. He casually asked Aubrey what he was up to and Aubrey said that he was "Adjusting my plans around young Jason." It was good to hear that Aubrey had plans.

Yeats had stopped by to drop off their personal belongings and had apparently brought Aubrey up to speed on the goings-on with the Red Feather Gang.

Will had a shower, changed his clothes and immediately felt better.

When Harley went in for her shower, Will sat down on the back patio that overlooked the quarry in the distance, and sipped a very tart ginger beer Aubrey served him in a tall glass full of ice.

Will looked at the moss hanging from the tree at the back of the property. Aubrey said it was called "old man's beard."

"Why were you hoping not to come home the other day? The day you saved us when we were being chased. Was it because of your son Anthony's death?" Will asked, not quite believing he was being so bold.

Aubrey chased an ice cube with his index finger before saying, "I thought my world was built around my son. But in truth it was built around a belief about my son. A belief that didn't square with the truth. When I heard he was killed and had killed another man because of his reckless pursuit of pleasure, well, my world crumbled, Will."

Sensing that emotions were running high, Hamlet slinked under the table and thumped the table leg with his tail.

"Who's a good boy, who's a good boy? You are, Hammy, Hamlet. Yes, yes," said Aubrey, splaying his rake-like fingers and ruffling the dog's coat. "Who's a good-looking beast, hmmm? Yes, yes, that's what the world needs is more good-looking beasts."

When Aubrey looked up, Will still fixed him in his gaze, not allowing the interlude with the dog to take his question off the table.

"I made a deal with God. I said that if I had worn out my time here on earth, I would let him sweep me out to sea. Instead, He swept you and Harley to me."

Aubrey cast a sad look back at the family home then brought it back to the ocean that lapped at the old concrete dock down the path.

"See, Will, I had an idea of who I was, what I had made of myself. And it was bound up with who I thought my son was. He had taken to drinking and driving on a regular basis and I didn't know it. So it was just a question of time before ... But after I heard what had happened, I realized I wasn't what I believed myself to be. I was a shrinking man."

Will cleared the catch from his voice and said, "Well, Aubrey, that may be but I can distinguish between who you are and who your son was. I like you and I don't like your son. I hate him for what he's done to you."

"You didn't know my son so you can't say you don't like him."

"He's making you shrink."

"Children don't think of the impact their decisions and actions will have upon themselves and others. It's called 'inconsequential thinking' because they don't think of the consequences, about how it will impact their parents, their families, others. It's a short-coming. Can't hate a person for that."

"Okay, Aubrey. I'll stop hating him if you stop shrinking. Deal?" Will thrust his hand out to shake on it. "Promise?"

"All right, Will, I won't shrink anymore. I won't go into the water and I won't shrink anymore." Aubrey blinked back the sadness and inched his hand up until his big, powerful stonecutter's hand swallowed Will's.

"You hear that, Hamlet? You're going to be able to keep nesting on Aubrey's pillow," said Will, his voice faltering as he fought back a tear.

That night the tree frogs gave him more encouragement than he needed with their cry to sleep, sleep, sleep.

Chapter Eighteen

A Moving Disguise

*Banyan tree: Also called a Ficus tree, it has the unusual habit of
sending a mesh of secondary roots to the ground from its branches.*

Will knew he'd slept late by the intensity of the sun prying its
way through the bamboo blinds. Harley's bed had been made.
He hadn't heard a thing and thought he hadn't moved after his
head had hit the pillow right after they'd finished the steamed
red snapper. Will made for the kitchen.

There was a bowl on the table with two, still tepid, boiled eggs
and toast waiting for him. Will disposed of each egg in two
mouthfuls, then pinched a piece of toast and stepped outside.
The screen door clacked behind him. He took a bite from the
toast and waved to Harley, who was sorting clothes in the laundry
room that backed onto the house.

The slingshot he'd found in Aubrey's son's room was lying on
the table. Aubrey had replaced the sagging rubber with a strip
of bicycle tire inner tube. There were a handful of palm grapes
nestled up against it. Will couldn't resist shooting one of the hard
palm grapes into the air. He watched it arc its way through the
humid air and whack a large palm frond.

A persistent scraping noise from the far back of Aubrey's

property drew his attention. He looked at Harley, who shrugged.

Will dropped some grapes into his left cargo pocket to balance the cellphone he had in the right pocket. He ambled out into the sunshine in pursuit of the source of the scraping sound, shooting grapes here and there with the slingshot as he went.

He found Aubrey, his T-shirt speckled with perspiration, drawing a saw through a block of stone. The long saw blade bristled with big, widespread teeth, unlike the fine-tooth wood saws his father used. Will assumed the spacing between the teeth worked better on the soft Bermuda stone.

Will watched Aubrey saw through a two-inch-thick slice and wipe his forehead with a handkerchief. He waved Will over. "This is what the first island houses were made of. Many still are. And the best quality stone is kept for roofing. Early Bermudians were quick to understand that a stone roof has a better chance of surviving a hurricane than, say, a thatched roof. It also allows us to gather water into the cisterns that are found under most houses on the island."

"So," said Will with a grin, "You just decided to come out and saw stone to remind yourself of how you used to do things?"

"No, because I believe there's a market for hand-cut stone … and I may be doing this for a living again," replied Aubrey in a quiet voice.

"You mean on top of your water company and the stone-cutting company you already own?"

Aubrey leaned his hips against the big block of stone and stared at the ground. "See, Will, when I thought I wasn't coming back, before we met on the ocean, before I promised you I wouldn't shrink anymore, well I gave away my two companies. One went to the family of the boy my son killed when he hit him with my truck and the other to my workers who've been with me since forever."

Will shook his head. "You mean, you gave away your means of living?"

"Well, Will, I wasn't planning on needing them, now, was I? And before you get into it, no, I can't undo it. My lawyer warned me it would be a done deal, irrevocable-like. And even if I could, to tell them that I'd made, well, let's call it a mistake, well now that would be a heartbreak I'm not prepared to inflict on all of those good people. Been enough of that going 'round," explained Aubrey.

"But," protested Will, "You're a —."

Before he could complete his sentence, Harley crashed through the bushes.

"The Red Feather Gang," was all she managed to blurt between gasps, waving her hand in the direction of the house.

Will and Aubrey cocked an ear. A menacing chorus of scooters could be heard approaching, slowly so as not to alert their prey.

Will scrambled up the nearest banyan tree and, leaning onto his hands, made his way up a large branch, stepping from one split in the branches to another till he could see above the canopy.

Ten scooters snuck into Aubrey's lane. Although he couldn't see the color from this distance, Will knew that the tufts on the riders' helmets were red. They pulled their scooters onto their center stands, then, on Drury's signal, fanned out around the house.

Will retraced his path back down and splayed the fingers of both hands so they'd know there were ten gang members. "They've surrounded the house."

Aubrey looked back to his house. "Once they realize we're not there, they'll come looking for us back here. We need to get to the van."

"How can we get to the van without being seen?" asked Will.

They each searched around for a solution when Harley said,

"The old man's beard. We camouflage ourselves in that. Do you have your pocket knife?" she asked Aubrey.

When he handed it to her, she opened it and motioned for them to follow her into the woods. She cut strips of old man's beard down and slipped one of the stringy, green-gray tufts into each of Will's shirt pockets. Aubrey's face brightened in comprehension and he and Will joined Harley in stuffing his pockets and belt with strands of camouflage. They then knotted strands together and draped them over each other's heads as they heard the gang members getting closer.

Chapter Nineteen

Go Karts

*Dumbwaiter: A small elevator that carries items,
usually food, from one floor to another.*

Draped in old man's beard, Will, Harley, and Aubrey stood inside
the line of trees, and when members of the gang approached, they
froze behind the branches of the closest tree. With a light breeze,
the tufts of stringy lichen moved around just as it would on a tree.

When the gang members' attention was drawn away, the three
slipped farther along the trees toward the house, the lane and
closer to Aubrey's van, which promised their escape.

One of the gang members stopped to light a cigarette, apparently determined to just stay in front of them on the path instead
of moving.

As furtively as he could, Will pulled a few palm grapes from
his left pocket and the slingshot from his back pocket, loaded the
rubber band with a grape, and let it fly behind the gang member
as he exhaled smoke skyward.

Because he didn't pull it back very far the rubber didn't thwack
when he let it go. But thirty yards away, the olive-sized grape
smacked into leaves. The gang member flinched. He crouched
to peer into the trees on the other side of the clearing. But he

still didn't move. So Will shot another grape farther to the right. This time the gang member skipped over to where it had landed. The trio side-slid about twenty yards closer to the van.

The trees were neither big nor very thick along the driveway back to the house and van. If they went deeper into the thicker woods it would be impossible to make headway through the tangled foliage. Any minute now the gang would reach the back of the quarry and come back to search the return run.

They inched along, not giving in to their anxiety and not making any abrupt or long sprints, barely breathing. Will actually thought they'd make it. Their ruse had fooled everyone — except for Hamlet.

He waggled his way through the trees and rubbed up against Aubrey's leg, thumping his tail against his shinbone. Stepping away from the safety of the trees, the three scarecrows tiptoed to the van when a voice called out, "Going to a costume party, are you?" It was Drury, his lip curled back in a smile devoid of kindness. His right hand rested on the pistol in his belt.

"So, Will, Harley, we need you and we need that letter you've taken from us," said Drury, letting his pistol hang by his side.

Aubrey pulled the old man's beard free from his head and shirt collar. "Why are you picking on these children? What harm have they visited upon you that you'd threaten them like this?" he asked, stepping in front of Drury's gun.

"This doesn't concern you. It's between my boss and these two."

"You point a gun at my guests, on my property, and you've made it my concern, young man."

Harley put her hand on Aubrey's forearm. "I don't want you getting hurt now, Aubrey."

Drury frowned, looked at Aubrey, then at his truck with "Dill Enterprises" stenciled on the door before spinning around. "Are you Aubrey Dill, the cricket player?"

When nobody denied it, Drury enthused, "You're Bermuda's most famous cricketer. You held the highest individual score in the country for decades. My father told me all about you."

"Appears there were a few things your father didn't tell you that he should have. Manners being one of them."

Will pulled out the old cellphone, held it out toward Drury, and clicked on the buttons before saying, "Our friend Yeats knows about you being here, Drury. If you even point that gun at us again he'll have the police waiting before you can gather your gang and get to the bottom of the laneway."

Drury made a face. "Nice try, but I don't believe you, Will."

Will lifted the phone and said, "Hey Yeats, you watching all of this?"

Drury's look of disbelief morphed into serious concern when he heard, "You betcha."

"Think you can call the police and get them here before the Red Feather Gang takes us?"

Again the phone blurted, "You betcha."

"Okay, thanks Yeats," said Will, making a show of clicking off the non-existent connection.

Drury shot Will a venomous look, put two fingers to his mouth and blew a shrill whistle that brought the rest of the gang running. Drury signaled for them to get on their scooters and go. One of the gang members said something, and Drury barked, "Because I said so, is why."

After the last scooter disappeared around the bend, Will said, "I don't think Drury has spoken to Yeats, so he didn't know that was Humbert's voice."

Aubrey and Harley laughed and Harley grabbed Will in a bear hug and spun him around till he was laughing too.

She stopped to catch her breath. "I think we have to go on the offensive and stop running away from them."

"The fact that you haven't found *Wavelength* tells me they've either done a great job of hiding her or possibly even scuttled her," said Aubrey.

"Don't you find it strange that they keep chasing us?" asked Will.

"They want that letter back," said Harley.

"They know the content of the letter," argued Will. "But they keep chasing us, which is a lot riskier than leaving us alone because we have no proof of their involvement. We're missing something here," said Will.

After a moment to let this sink in, Will said, "You remember when Drury was talking to Bennett on *Wavelength* and he mentioned other letters?" Harley nodded. "Well I think we keep looking for the boat but we should try to find and read those other letters."

Harley nodded. "So where do we look for those letters?"

"I think we should try Brian Ord's place. The one I saw on Front Street, just past where the cruise ships dock. I saw Ord and Claire on the upstairs patio."

Harley pursed her lips. "Well, that makes sense, but if Brian Ord's involved in this, he's not going to just let us waltz in there. And if you're right, there are going to be gang members around so it won't be easy."

Hamlet came out of the bushes and looked from one human to the other as if he too was looking for an answer. Will leaned over and patted his back as the big tail whacked his legs.

Aubrey glanced at his watch and said, "I know how we can get inside. Will, please give Yeats a call." They plucked the remaining strands of old man's beard off, jumped into the van and drove to the races.

Yeats led them through the crowds lining the go-kart course along Hamilton's Front Street. Like the rest of the Windy Farm volunteers, Will, Harley, and Aubrey wore the blue Windy Farm hats, shirts, and pants and had the orange reflector vests like the security personnel wore around the track. The go-karts were a few minutes away from their practise runs and the drivers in their fireproof suits milled about their karts with their respective crews who used the parking lot as a collective pit stop.

The stage on the waterfront side to the left of the go-karts erupted with the sounds of trumpets, drums and strident whistles as a troupe of Gombeys strode out in a circular procession, then appeared to rush the audience brandishing bows and arrows or wooden snakes. When they scooted past Will, he noticed that their masks were made up of mesh crisscrossed with tape. Locals and tourists alike took pictures.

Will, Harley, and Aubrey stopped now and again to help Yeats push a straw bale into a tighter formation or to politely ask parents not to let children stand on them.

Like other stores on the main drag, the Ord Gallery had a sign in the window that said, "Closed for the races," but Brian Ord and Claire Calloway had not left. Will bobbed his chin upward. Harley looked to the second floor balcony to see Claire come out to where Brian Ord sat in his wheelchair. She leaned in, but because he had his sun-blocking gauze on his face, it was hard to tell if he was talking or listening. She waved to someone in the crowd before wheeling him back inside.

Members of the Red Feather Gang in their white jackets loitered in front of the door to the gallery. But as the go-karts started their warm-up laps, they stepped forward, away from the open door, crowding the bales in order to get a closer look.

As soon as the performance was over, the Gombeys headed for the backstage area. So did Aubrey, Will, and Harley. The spectators turned their gaze to the racecourse.

No one paid attention to the tall Gombey and two shorter ones as they edged around the crowd. They passed by the blue food tents that were doing brisk business. A very large woman to whom people yelled orders like, "Louise, two more jerk chickens," managed the food tent closest to the sidewalk.

Even though he could see through the Gombey costume's mesh mask, it wasn't perfectly clear and took some getting used to. So did the unexpected weight of the three-foot-tall hat adorned with fluttering feathers.

They waited for the sound of approaching go-karts before scooting across the sidewalk. When the crowd started to "ooh" and "ah" and a cart skidded into the bale wall and spun out in a burst of smoking tires, the gang members whooped and craned forward to see. That's when Aubrey waved them through the open door and upstairs.

At the top of the stairs, they followed the hall to their right when they heard a woman yelling, "You go out and find those kids and bring them and the letter they stole or the same thing that happened to Bennett will happen to you."

The door down the hall flew open and Drury scooted out, making sure to close the door behind him. He looked up, saw the three Gombeys and snarled, "What the hell are you doing up here?"

Drury strode toward them. "I said, what the hell are you doing up here?"

Will and Harley froze. Aubrey stepped forward and lowered his voice by an octave. That and the muffling effect of the mask made Aubrey's voice unrecognizable. "I'm just looking for the restaurant bathroom for my kids."

"That's next door," Drury answered in a calmer voice and flicked his thumb over his shoulder.

"Right, thanks," mumbled Aubrey, "come on kids, let's get next door then." He fluttered his gloved hands forward like he was coaxing chickens back to their roost.

Drury rushed past them on the stairs. By the time they skipped out the door and turned left, Drury was pulling his gang together in a huddle.

A few minutes later, shed of the Gombey costumes they had borrowed from people Aubrey knew, Will and Harley followed Aubrey past Louise's blue food tent. They hurried up to the restaurant's second floor balcony next door to Brian Ord's building. Will kept thinking about what they'd heard Claire Calloway say: "Or the same thing that happened to Bennett will happen to you." What had happened to Bennett?

Because he knew the restaurant owner, Aubrey was able to get three chairs placed behind the tables at the front corner, just ahead of a concrete wall. Here they didn't block anyone's view. Better still, unlike the tables in front of the windows, they weren't on display for the Red Feather Gang to spot them.

Will got up and pretended to be interested in the race below. With the sunglasses on he looked just like an eager spectator. But keeping his head straight and his eyes to the right, he saw that Brian Ord's second floor balcony was empty.

The security divider from the restaurant balcony to Ord's building was in the shape of a fantail or a sun whose rays were made of sharp, steel, javelin-like rods where rust marks leeched through the faded yellow paint.

Will stole a glance through the rays. The blinds on the large windows to Ord's balcony had not been closed. Will saw the outline of a woman as she pulled a bundle of keys from a desk drawer. She shouldered her purse, opened the door, then used a key to lock the door behind her. Claire Calloway hadn't seen him.

The crowd rose to its feet as two go-kart engines shattered the briny air with barely muffled motors racing toward this neck of the course. When they came to the turn, they bumped and the crowd roared in either support or dismay.

Will slipped a foot onto one of the sun's rays. He felt it slacken under his weight, then he sprang up and around the sharp points. He backed along the concrete wall to be sure he wasn't seen from across the street. Will pushed the unlocked patio door open and took a few tentative steps into the office.

There was a computer monitor on the big desk facing the ocean and a large TV mounted on the wall. The cupboards at the back of the wall were made of well-varnished, honey-hued Bermuda cedar.

The one thing missing from the office was Brian Ord. On the side table at the back, Will saw a stack of gauze gloves and face masks that Dr. Doan had said Ord used because of his skin cancer. Will pulled on a pair of gloves so he wouldn't leave fingerprints. The wastepaper basket was filled with sunflower seed shells that had been spat there. Dr. Doan had said it was one of Ord's peculiar habits.

With the gloves on, he tried the desk drawers. The center one was locked. The four side drawers contained the usual stuff from an office desk: a stapler, a scotch tape dispenser, paper clips, note pads, pens, pencils, erasers. But there was no old letter from Papineau Benoit.

He sat in the big leather chair and swiveled this way and that as he pondered his next move. A breeze swayed the blinds back into the room and something fluttered and caught his eye. He pulled himself out of the chair and went to one of the wall panels where he found a piece of gauze wedged. He tugged on it and the strand came out a tiny bit, then refused to move further. How could someone have managed to shove it so far into the panel and why? Unless it was caught there.

When he pushed on the panel it sprang back. He stifled a scream. The panel was a floor to ceiling piece that opened on a big dumbwaiter elevator.

When it sprang open, a light came on. There was a lit-up panel on the inside that had buttons to the basement and floors one and two.

He stepped into the box and pressed on the "B." A very faint whirr could be heard from below and he was carried down at a very slow pace.

It came to a stop with a faint shudder and a click. He pushed the brass handle and the door swung open. He didn't realize that the lift hadn't stopped at a completely level surface, so he caught his toe on the lip, sprawled forward, and landed on his stomach.

He shook his head at the smell of decay, looked up and screamed. He was staring into the gauzed face of Brian Ord sitting in his wheelchair, his head tilted to one side, staring at him through his sunglasses.

Chapter Twenty

Dead Men Tell No Tales

Mummified: The state of a body preserved and shrunken
due to embalming or drying out.

When Will sprawled out of the elevator, the old phone Dr. Doan had lent them flew from his pocket. It clattered out in front of him and slid till it touched one of the front wheels on Ord's wheelchair. The man just stared straight ahead.

Will pulled himself onto his knees, forced himself to breathe and snatched his phone back. He turned it on but the reception wasn't strong enough in the basement.

Ord didn't know that. So Will sat back on his haunches and pretended to make a call. He stood as he dialed and tried to act as casual as possible by taking a few steps to the left. Ord's head didn't swivel to follow his movements. Was he that cool, that sure that Will was his prisoner?

"That's a dummy," croaked a voice. Will jumped and brought up his hands defensively.

"It's a dummy, a mannequin, so it can't hurt you," said the voice, "and I can't hurt you either, Will."

Bennett. The voice belonged to Bennett and it was coming through an open door to a darkened room on the left. Will turned and walked to Ord and pulled the gauze back to reveal a plastic mannequin face.

Will tiptoed over to the open door, ready to bolt to the elevator if he needed to. He felt for the light switch and flicked it on.

The room was full of paintings. Every inch of every wall was covered in paintings. Most of them were framed but some stretched-canvas pieces were leaning against each other here and there.

In the back of the room, Bennett, or Benoit, or whatever his real name was, slumped forward in his chair. He blinked away at the unexpected brightness. Will held his breath. Will could see blood had dripped onto his soiled, white shirt.

"Mr. Bennett?" said Will.

Bennett sat up and Will saw that his arms were handcuffed behind his back, secured to the chair's steel frame.

"Can you help me get out of here, Will? Please. She'll kill me if she can. She's crazy," blurted Bennett.

Inching closer, Will saw that Bennett's face was cut. His bruises had taken on yellow and purple hues so they weren't fresh.

He blurted, "She's gone, but when she gets back, she'll finish me off. I know it."

"Who are you talking about, Mr. Bennett?" interrupted Will.

"Claire. Claire Calloway of course. Who else? She's the master-mind of this whole thing," said Bennett, shaking his head at Will's lack of understanding.

"I thought she worked for Brian Ord," said Will.

"She did when I met Ord six months ago. When I showed him the painting."

"What painting?" asked Will.

Bennett took a breath to calm himself. "There, see those two, almost identical paintings of the blockade runner in the middle of the wall?"

Bennett motioned toward the paintings to urge Will to go over, which he did. The identical paintings were signed *Edward James*. Both had his little cameo of his goateed self sitting on a hill, painting as a screw steamer at anchor was firing up its boilers. The two frames bore the inscription, "H.M.S. *Lily* in St. George Harbour, 1863."

"Okay, now that you've seen them, please help get me free," pleaded Bennett.

"No. Not until you explain what this is about. You kidnapped Harley and me and tried to kill us. So no, I'm not doing anything till you explain what's going on," said Will, crossing his arms to show the determination he didn't really feel.

"For God's sake, Will, she's going to come back and kill me. And you too if she finds you here."

"Then you'd better talk fast," urged Will.

"That painting on the left belonged to Papineau Benoit, my great, great grandfather. When my grandmother died seven months ago I inherited her house. In the attic, amidst a ton of junk, I found this painting, which I thought was worthless. Until I found the letters."

"Papineau Benoit's letters? The ones he'd sent to his wife?" asked Will.

Bennett shook his head, yes. "Most of the letters were just about day-to-day things, but then I found four that seemed to indicate that money, a considerable sum of money had been made during the Civil War while he was here. And one letter in particular spoke of money that disappeared during the shipwreck of Papineau's blockade runner off the coast of Bermuda."

"The one he named *Lily*, after his wife?" asked Will.

"Yes, yes," Bennett snapped with impatience. "So I read about this guy, Edward James in the letters. His paintings have a certain worth among those who collect Bermudian paintings."

"That's how you came to contact Brian Ord, because he owned the art gallery?"

Bennett nodded. "Ord asked me why I wanted to sell it. I took a chance and told him I wanted to raise enough capital to do a wreck dive for *Lily* because, based on my ancestor's letters, I had a good idea where she'd sunk. I didn't think he'd believe me. But he took me here and showed me the twin to my painting. His was the one that Consul Allen sent to the navy. So Ord knew of *Lily* and he wanted to hear about the content of Papineau's letters. We agreed to split whatever we found fifty/fifty."

Before continuing, Bennett shot a worried look toward the back room, then to the open elevator he could see through the door. "Turns out our Mr. Ord was not only selling original paintings. He was involved in forged paintings as well. And he and his father had shown a certain skill in buying up recovered treasure. That is, until the Bermudian government passed a law claiming all sunken treasure in territorial waters as part of their national heritage."

"Is that why you wanted to smuggle wreck-excavating equipment into Bermuda?"

"Yes. I dove and within a week I'd found the wreck based on the geography mentioned in Papineau's last letter. All we needed was the underwater excavating gear. I'm sorry Will. You were just supposed to bring the boat here and fly home. We didn't count on you and Harley finding the gear in that hollowed-out water tank. I wasn't even worried that you had found our excavation gear because you didn't know what it was for. But Claire didn't want to take any chances. She wanted us to make it look like an accident. Probably what she had in store for me. Dead men tell no tales."

"You keep saying 'her.' Isn't Brian Ord behind all of this?" pressed Will.

Bennett again shook his head with impatience and large drops of blood flew off the end of his nose and landed on Will's pants. He tried to rub them off but they smeared, like two big wounds on either thigh.

"I called Ord from Nova Scotia and told him you and your cousin were bringing the boat here. He said he didn't like involving children and would think about the deal. Never saw him again. Claire wanted him to stick with the plan to try and find the shipwreck. They argued and he had a heart attack and she let him die. When I got back here, he was already dead — only I didn't know that till just the other day."

"Wait a minute. I just saw Mr. Ord on the balcony," protested Will.

"That's the dummy you saw in the other room. She dresses it up like Ord so she can wheel him out there and leans in pretending to talk to him so people who walk by on the street think he's still alive. She even spits sunflower seed shells into waste bins like Ord did when he was alive. That's how sick she is. As his manager she was already running just about everything for him, so taking over from Ord after his death wasn't that difficult for her."

Will shook his head. "It wasn't a dummy I saw on the Boston Whaler when he came out to *Wavelength*," blurted Will.

"I thought it was Ord too. But it was Claire. See, he was pretty frail at the end, so he and Claire were about the same size. After he died, Claire just wore his clothes and with that gauze he always had on his face and hands to protect against the sun, well, she looked the part. And when she was on the boat, she only talked to us by cellphone and lowered her voice."

"So she's the one who gave the order to 'make it look like an accident' on the boat?" asked Will. "That's why she kept sending the gang after us. Not because she needed the content of the letter but because our story could bring the police here and they would discover what she'd done with Ord."

Bennett nodded, again flinging blood from his nose. "She was boiling mad that I'd lost that letter at the archives. She said I had put them all at risk. That we'd be found out — not just the illegal wreck diving but all that stolen stuff Ord was involved in," he said, nodding to the back room. "Of course, at that time, Drury and I didn't know she had let him die. Drury still doesn't know Ord's dead."

Bennett caught his breath, then continued, "After she threatened me, I realized I had to get away. Before she could read them, I hid two letters on the boat, wrapped in plastic. When I snuck down here to get my painting back, I stumbled onto the room full of stuff stolen by the Red Feather Gang. I heard her coming. I tried to hide in that closet. And that's how I found him. I screamed. She pulled out a gun and told me I knew far too much."

"You're saying she left him to die in that closet?" asked Will.

"Yes, yes. If you don't believe me, open the door and see for yourself."

Will sidestepped toward the closet and laid his hand on the handle. He held his breath and jerked it open. He jumped back. Inside the cupboard, in his wheelchair, sat Brian Ord — or what was left of him. There was a bit of skin showing between the gauze gloves and his shirt cuff. Ord was mummified, and this was where the slight smell of decay was coming from.

"And now you know too so we're both at risk. Please, Will, find something to cut me loose. I'm not the one to worry about, she is. Please," said Bennett with exasperation.

Will leapt to the back room and flicked the light on. He stopped cold. The room was jammed up with all kinds of items: flat screen televisions, laptops, cellphones, two scooters, at least six gas generators, jewelry in a series of baskets and pillow cases full of stuff just piled onto and under foldout tables.

Will skipped over to a counter and pulled a number of drawers open till he found a pair of pliers and ran back to Bennett.

"Was Claire the one who hooked up with the Red Feather Gang?" asked Will.

He knelt beside Bennett and he turned his wrist toward Will.

"No, that was Brian Ord. Two years ago he was approached by that guy Drury who had stolen a painting. Ord realized these guys needed organizing and a place to stash their loot and if need be, sit on it till the police lost interest, then sell it, sometimes by shipping things to the Caribbean. He had the money to pay them a deposit and the patience to wait it out before selling it," explained Bennett.

"What changed?" asked Will. He squeezed on the pliers to get its pinchers to bite into the chain on the handcuff. Nothing. Again he squeezed as hard as he could till he heard a crack. One of the pliers' jaws had snapped off.

Bennett's head sagged with despair. "She's been counting on us finding Papineau Benoit's treasure then getting out of Bermuda before anybody realizes what's up. She was probably going to cut me out of the picture all along."

"It's worth that much?" asked Will.

"Papineau wrote he'd been paid in US double eagles. They were worth twenty dollars back then. But if they're in good shape, Ord thought that they could be worth over two million dollars as collector pieces."

"Why hasn't she taken the money and left?" asked Will. "You found the wreck. That's why we were diving there —"

"The money box was empty. Drury and I did a night dive but found nothing. Papineau's done something else with the gold. That's why I was looking at the archives. For a place called Trotters' Trail. But —" said Bennett, freezing in mid-sentence.

They heard an electric garage door opening somewhere in the

back of the building. A car rumbled into the garage. Its motor stopped. Will shot a look at Bennett, who had gone pale.

"That's her. She's back. Get outta here before she gets you too."

"I can't just leave you," hissed Will, looking off to the far door that he assumed led to the underground garage.

"Go and get help. If she finds you here, we're both dead. She's got a gun, Will, and she'll use it. When you get back up to the office, look in a file drawer for one called 'Edward James.' That's where you'll find one of Papineau's letters. That's the one that led me to the wreck," said Bennett. "Now go, go."

Will scurried into the elevator and stabbed the second floor button. This time the whirr sounded incredibly loud, probably because he knew Claire Calloway had entered the basement.

The elevator hadn't fully stopped on the second floor landing before Will bolted out and over to the desk. He yanked the lower drawer open, running his finger along the files till he came to the one marked "Edward James."

He flipped it open, ignored the photocopies of his various paintings but stopped when he saw the old-time envelope addressed from Papineau to Lily. He heard the elevator start up. Claire Calloway was on her way here.

Will jammed the letter into his shirt pocket. He slid against the desk smudging it with Bennett's blood that had landed on his pants. Once on the balcony, Will slowed his pace as he sidled along the concrete wall till he was abreast of the sunburst guard-rail. He threw one last look at the hidden elevator panel and as soon as the first go-kart screeched through the turn below, Will hoisted himself out onto the same steel rods he'd used to spin onto Brian Ord's patio.

This time the rusted rod under his foot didn't sag. It snapped. Will fell backward with a scream that was drowned out by the go-kart engines.

Chapter Twenty-one

Papineau's Last Letter

Capstan: A nautical apparatus used for hoisting heavy objects such as anchors, by means of a line around a vertical spool-shaped cylinder that is rotated manually or by motor.

Will waved his arms in a vain attempt to stop his fall. He did a perfect back flop into the blue food tent before passing out.

He didn't know how long he'd been out. He could hear the go-karts racing off in the distance, but nearby voices were pushing their way into his consciousness. He blinked awake and stared into the worried, round face of Louise, the large woman serving up Jamaican food from inside the tent.

"Well, sweetie, lucky for you my broad back was under the tent when you decided to go Olympic diving on us. I know my jerk chicken be the best on the island but you didn't hav'ta go to that length to get yo'sef some," she said, smiling.

"Will! Will, are you okay?" asked Harley, peering over Louise's shoulder.

"Excuse me, please. I'm a doctor. Please, just let me have a look at — oh my God, it's Will," said Dr. Doan, her face shifting from professional poise to concern, then back to business mode.

"I think I'm okay," said Will, trying to pull himself upright.

"Just you lie there a moment till I have a look at you —" said Dr. Doan before she was interrupted by another voice.

"Excuse me, please let us through. Police. Please move back and, oh, Dr. Doan, what have we got here, then?" asked a Bermudian police officer in blue polo shirt and matching cargo pants as he kneeled beside Dr. Doan. He looked at Will's pants and added, "You're bleeding. Do we need an ambulance?"

"It's not my blood," wheezed Will, still trying to get his breath back.

The officer leaned into the walkie-talkie hanging on his left shoulder, activated the two-way radio, and said, "Hey, Mickey, tie her up and join me here in front of the Ord Gallery, will you?" He turned back to Will. "I'm Sergeant Wilson. Where did this blood come from, and how did it end up on you?"

Will used the officer's hand to pull himself into a sitting position. He leaned out around the tent and peered between the legs of the onlookers who were staring down at him.

"I was up there on the restaurant patio and I could see a woman hitting Mr. Ord in his wheelchair on his patio. I think she was using a gun," lied Will, wanting to warn the officer. Will knew the Bermudian police weren't armed so he didn't want Sergeant Wilson to walk into a shooting situation. "She pushed him inside and he was bleeding. You know, up against the desk. The big desk in there. So I ran in to help, but she had pushed him into an elevator. He needs help. Dr. Doan, he needs help, in the basement. He's there bleeding. And he needs help now."

"What makes you think they were going to the basement?" asked the sergeant.

"Uh, well, I, I …," began Will, looking to Harley for help. She held up her hands to show Will she had bunched up the gauze gloves in one hand and had pulled Papineau's letter from his pocket and held it in her other hand.

Reassured he wasn't about to be exposed as a break-in thief, Will regained his composure. "Well, I think the gallery's closed today because of the race. So that floor's closed and I'm guessing she took him to the basement, wouldn't you think, Sergeant?"

Another officer made his way through the crowd. Sergeant Wilson turned and said to him, "We're going to have a look on the second floor balcony of the Ord building to see if there's someone there in need of assistance. And Mickey, there's a report of a gun on the premises."

With Dr. Doan's warning that Will wasn't to overdo it, the two officers and Will retraced his steps from the restaurant's balcony to Ord's balcony. Will was told to stay on the restaurant balcony. Most of the guests barely took time from the go-kart race below to pay them the slightest interest.

"Police officers. Who's in there?" Sergeant Wilson called into the office. When no answer came, they pushed their way through the door.

"The elevator's right there," said Will, pointing.

When the officers followed the direction he was pointing, Will swiveled from the patio he was on to the Ord patio. Before they could protest, Will skipped past them to the hidden elevator.

"They went in here," said Will, giving the panel a little shove so that it sprang back. The officers stared into the darkness. Without explaining how he knew to do it, Will clicked the button that whirred the elevator back up to them.

The two officers got in and disappeared. A few minutes later they emerged looking pale and serious. "Well, someone's been handcuffed to a chair down there. Blood splats everywhere. And Mr. Ord is dead. It couldn't have been him you saw because the body we found in a wheelchair's been dead for quite a while," explained Sergeant Wilson.

"But not long enough for the smell to completely dissipate," said the other officer, who looked pale.

Sergeant Wilson said, "We also saw a whole bunch of paintings and what looks like a lot of stolen goods. We've called in the criminal investigation unit."

"What about the man I saw in the wheelchair? He was alive and he needs your help and, well, you have to do something to help him, don't you?"

"Well, there's also a mannequin that looks like Brian Ord in a wheelchair in the basement. But I can't imagine she'd hit a mannequin. And it wasn't a mannequin that bled all over the floor down there. I've called in Claire Calloway's description. We'll bring her in for questioning. You up to giving us a statement, Will?" asked Sergeant Wilson.

"Uh, well, you know, sure, I'd like to. But right now I feel I'd like to just lie down, if that's all right. Not feeling too good. Seeing all that blood, you know."

"Sure, sure," said Wilson, ushering them all back out to the balcony and the fresh breeze. "Let's get you back to your family and Dr. Doan, shall we?"

They drove back to Aubrey's place and ate the jerk chicken meals Louise insisted on giving them because she'd never had a client drop in like Will had to get her food before. There'd been enough excitement for one day, so they ate in silence. Aubrey insisted Harley stay with Will as he cleaned up the dinner dishes.

"Hey, Harley," whispered Will, despite the fact that the only ones listening were the keskidees perched on the nearby branches, "let's read Papineau's letter, huh? According to Bennett, Ord thought the gold coins could be worth over two million dollars. That would make up for Aubrey giving away his companies, right?"

Harley nodded, unfolded the letter and read it out loud.

St. George, Bermuda, July 30, 1864

My dearest Lily:

I can scarcely believe that I am alive and penning this letter from Trotters' Trail. A few days ago I would have been hard-pressed to imagine this possible.

A month ago we were at anchor in St. George, awaiting a cargo that needed shipping. I was having dinner at the Globe Hotel when in came Villiers Rougemont with a man he introduced as Dr. Luke Blackburn. They bade me accompany them along Penno's Wharf as they had a delicate business proposition they wished to put to me.

Dr. Blackburn tells me he has trunks full of clothes he wishes brought to auction in Boston. They called upon my dedication to the Southern cause to take these trunks but not to open them or to come into contact with the clothes, this under any circumstances. Blackburn was reticent but Villiers, who had been drinking, bragged that the clothes belonged to those who had succumbed to Yellow Jack and had been collected by Dr. Blackburn who had ministered to them. Because the textile mills have been closed for want of cotton, used clothes have gone up in value. Once auctioned in Boston, they believe the infected clothes will ravage the north with yellow fever and do what Lee's armies have not done: annihilate the north by attacking civilians.

Harley skimmed bits and summarized. Papineau refused the offer and thought it was the end of the issue — it wasn't. Days later, Papineau was hired at the last minute to take salted meat and two new Whitworth breech-loading, rifled cannons to Wilmington. Unable to assemble his crew on time, Papineau and his partners accepted the men the new client provided. Papineau had just paid off his debts, bought a Bermudian cottage called

Trotters' Trail and hired Edward James to paint a fresco of the family over the fireplace. His payment for this trip was two thousand dollars in double eagle coins that filled his wooden money box. This payment ensured it would be his last trip as a blockade runner. But all was not as it seemed.

They snuck into Charleston where, because of the previous outbreak of yellow fever, they were put in quarantine and overheard their replacement crew's real plan: take control of the ship and kill the partners. When cornered, the youngest mutineer admitted that they were hired by Villiers Rougemont to kill Papineau because he knew too much about Dr. Blackburn and Alexander Keith Jr.'s plans to spread yellow fever through the northern states. Papineau devised his own plan. Harley read:

> *Claiming routine maintenance, we started the boilers at sunset. I wrapped myself in layers of clothing and moved about my cabin until drenched in perspiration. Shedding the clothes, I came on deck and looked feverish to the mutineers. I spat out a mixture of fine coffee grounds and red wine as though vomiting dark blood — a sure sign I had the dreaded yellow fever. The mutineers panicked, jumped overboard, and swam for shore.*
>
> *One mutineer had not fallen for the ruse. He forced me at gunpoint to open the money box. We struggled; his gun went off, the bullet piercing his forehead. I did not have the luxury of removing his body.*

"That's the skeleton we found on the wreck," said Harley before skimming and summarizing the letter.

With all lights extinguished and with only a half load of cotton, Papineau risked running aground by leaving on the outgoing tide instead of the incoming tide when the Union Navy expected a run. Papineau loaded the cannons they hadn't delivered and fired blanks into the night, looking like they were part of the Union

Navy: blockade runners were unarmed so as not to be treated as combatants. Eventually the Union Navy got wise and fired their cannons. One ball wedged itself in a cotton bale but one hit the rudder. When *Lily's* rudder was damaged, Papineau steered with his twin propellers. Then the mutineers' cheap coal robbed the steam engines of so much power that they hit a reef during the stormy passage. Papineau wanted to run the boat ashore but his comrades chose to launch the longboat. Within a mile of the coast, he hit the second reef and swam for shore, where he shivered in the rain till morning so he could be sure of where she'd sunk, a mile out from the boilers. He rented a salvage tug and manned it himself. Harley again read:

Sadly, my five partners' upturned longboat was found wedged between shore rocks, two bodies washed ashore, weighed down by their gold coins.

From the salvage tug I was able to see my beloved Lily lying forty feet below the surface at low tide. I hooked my anchor to her railing, dove with a rope to the cannons and tied them off before winching them back up with the steam-powered capstan.

When the dockworkers in port saw me transfer the cannons to a horse-drawn carriage and realized that I had not brought up my money box, they thought I'd taken leave of my senses. I say, "Je répondrai par la bouche de mes cannons."

My suspicions about Villiers were confirmed when he saw me riding with the driver heading to Trotters' Trail. With one hand on his double-barreled derringer tucked into his belt, he staggered backwards into the pub like he'd seen a ghost.

I dine with Consul Allen tonight and will ask him to post this letter with the first packet heading to Halifax.

Kiss our son for me.

Your loving husband, Papineau.

Harley pointed at a sentence in the letter, saying, "He says here that he didn't salvage the money box, the wooden one we found on the wreck. I think he left the money box on the wreck because he knew it was empty. But he took the cannons back to Trotters' Trail. That's his cottage, right? Maybe he took the money there too, and just didn't want to say so in the letter in case somebody opened and read it before it reached his wife."

Will nodded, saying, "Bennett said he and Claire had tried to find Trotters' Trail but nobody knew it." As they headed for bed Harley said, "I wonder if we'll find it before she does."

Chapter Twenty-two

Night Dive

*Horsepower: A unit of power that generates 550 foot-pounds
per second, and adopted in the late 1800s by the Scottish engineer
James Watt who compared the power generated by a steam engine
to that of draft horses. A ten horsepower engine generates
the power of ten draft horses, or 5,500 foot-pounds per second.*

The cellphone rang once in the dark before Will grabbed it off the night table.

"Yes?" he whispered, scooting out of the room so as not to wake Harley.

"Will, it's Sherman. I think I've found *Wavelength*. I'm at Aubrey's dock if you and Harley want to come and confirm it's her."

Will said that he'd be right out. He let Harley sleep, hopped into his shorts and shoes before hurrying out of the house and to the far end of the dock where Sherman's fishing boat bobbed on the moonlit ocean. Will jumped aboard.

"Thanks for coming, Will."

"You call the police?" asked Will.

"Want you to confirm it for me before I do. Not far from here," he said, spinning the fishing boat around into its own wake. Will clambered up to the flying bridge and sat beside Sherman.

"You didn't wake Harley?"

"Thought she needed to sleep. Figured that's why you didn't call Aubrey."

Sherman nodded. They motored along as the sound of wind and waves kept them company. What Will didn't say, was that he'd also been thinking about his father's death. How much of a loss that had been when his father died of a heart attack a year ago. He'd grown fond of Aubrey and he feared that, like his father, he would also die — that the episode on the boiler was somehow a forewarning.

They slowed and Sherman pointed to a boat chugging along in the distance.

Will squinted at it. "That's not *Wavelength*."

Sherman stood to stare at the boat ahead. "They've un-stepped her mast and added some freeboard to change her outline." Sherman handed Will night vision goggles that allowed him to see the splintered remnants of the door to the hatchway that Drury had broken.

"You're right. It is her." Will looked again, "And that's Drury at the wheel."

Sherman nodded, staring at the boat making its way to open water. "And I'd venture they're not out here in the middle of the night collecting for the Red Cross, no sir, no sir."

Sherman called the Bermuda police on his cell in case Drury or Claire Calloway were listening to the radio's emergency frequency. He gave them their coordinates and the direction they were heading.

Just then, a smaller boat pounded its way across to *Wavelength*. "That's Claire Calloway," blurted Will. She came alongside *Wave-length* long enough for Drury to spring from the cockpit onto the smaller boat, which roared off, its twin props digging into the ocean for traction.

Wavelength continued its forward progress with no one at the helm. Sherman inched ahead till an explosion shattered the night.

Will saw the flash of light from *Wavelength*'s far side, and the thunderclap that followed buckled his knees and knocked him to the banquette. They stared at the fire that leaped as the motor, unaware of its death sentence, moved the craft dutifully forward, listing to starboard as water gushed into her ruptured hull.

Fearing a second explosion, Sherman kept his distance as *Wavelength* slipped below the surface, burbling air. A big air bubble escaped as they sailed over the very spot she'd occupied a few seconds ago. *Fathom*'s hull banged up against a horseshoe-shaped life-preserver. Will reached over to pick it up but dropped it when he saw it was still tied to the boat.

Then, from beneath the waves, Will heard banging and a muffled scream. Somebody was trapped in the wreck.

Before Will could say anything, P.C. Mickey Collin, with Sergeant Wilson by his side, raced the marine unit's Boston Whaler in close, her two hundred and twenty-five horsepower engines slowing to a throaty growl as she came smartly alongside Sherman's boat.

"Somebody's trapped aboard that boat that just blew up," yelled Will.

"We heard banging and muffled yells," said Sherman.

"It's gotta be Bennett," said Will.

Wilson gestured for Will to come aboard, yanked wetsuits from a locker and without looking up, asked, "You said you were a certified diver, Will? You prepared to dive down there with me and help me navigate inside? If there is an air pocket, seconds could make the difference between finding someone alive or dead."

They hurried into their wetsuits as Will cast a worried look into the dark water. Wilson added, "We'll have underwater lights." Will nodded, rolling the pant legs and sleeves back upon themselves.

Wilson led the way by leaping off the gunwale of the boat and hitting the water with a scissor kick. Will followed suit. They clicked on their two lights. When they turned the beams downward, they could clearly make out the sunken boat. Will followed Wilson down.

Everything slows down underwater, but it seemed to slow down even more at night. Wilson pulled the damaged door open and latched it in place so their exit wouldn't be blocked.

Will followed the policeman inside. It was as if they were on the space station with zero gravity. A magazine, liquid soap bottles, dishtowels, and paper napkins floated in the cabin as if trying to obscure something bad from their view. The explosion left a jagged hole where the gas stove had been. A few small, curious fish who were inside now darted back to the ocean, past the hull's splintered wood.

While Wilson made a U-turn toward Harley's bunk, Will, restricted by the narrowness of the cabin, small-kicked his flippers till he was in front of his room in the bow of the ship. He tried to open the door that had also been repaired, but it was locked. He reached up beside the sconce to the left of the door and unclipped the brass key. He leaned on the handle as he turned the key and the door pushed out toward him. A hand smacked Will's mask, and then he found himself looking into the bruised face of the man he feared he'd find.

Bennett's open eyes looked like they were begging for help — help that Will hadn't brought him in time. Wilson put his hand to Bennett's neck, feeling for the carotid artery. After what seemed like an eternity, with exhaled bubbles crowding the cabin, Wilson shook his head: there was no pulse. As Wilson pulled Bennett free, something fell away from the dead man's hand. Will picked it up: an old-style letter double-wrapped in plastic. He tucked it into the pocket of his BC vest.

Will was the first to bob at the surface. Wilson's head floated into the beam of light that P.C. Collin had brought.

"Give us a hand here, will ya Mickey?" said Wilson, dragging Bennett's body to the police boat. P.C. Collin hooked Bennett under the arm with a long gaff hook, brought him alongside, then, with a two-handed hoist, laid his body on the floor between the console and the air tank holder. He covered the body with a blanket.

Collins helped Will get aboard. When he got out of his BC vest, Will looked at the hand sticking out from under the blanket and asked, "Do you know how he died?" The fingernails looked to be broken, probably when he'd tried to claw his way out of the cabin as the water rose.

"We'll have to wait for the coroner's report," said Wilson. Bennett had been locked in the cabin and knew, when the explosion occurred, that his death was imminent and not going to be quick or pleasant, yet he still had the last of Papineau's letters with him, the last of Bennett's dream of finding his ancestor's gold coins.

Will watched with a feeling that he'd failed Bennett. Yes, he'd lied to them about the purpose of their trip, but did he deserve to be drowned by Claire Calloway? And he'd asked Will for help, which Will had failed to bring.

Wilson pulled out two bulky jackets from a locker. He and P.C. Collin put them on. Wilson answered Will's questioning look by saying, "A bullet-proof lifejacket. That Calloway woman just killed Bennett and she's armed," said Wilson, leaving the threat to hang about like the fumes from the big engines.

"You two be careful now," said Wilson as Will got back onto his fishing boat.

Wilson gave the motors gas, but not as much as he had to get there. Apparently, one rushed to save a life but not to bring back a dead body.

Would the letters he'd just found on *Wavelength* bring them any closer to Papineau's gold coins?

Chapter Twenty-three

A Graveyard Crawl

*Yellow fever: Also called Yellow Jack, it gets its name from the
jaundiced look of those infected by the mosquito-borne disease
that kills thirty thousand people annually, mostly in equatorial
areas where vaccines are in short supply. When it struck
Bermuda in the 1860s, it was inaccurately thought to
be transmitted by contact, like a cold or the flu.*

Harley and Aubrey were waiting for Will when Sherman dropped
him at Aubrey's house. They'd heard the explosion and Sherman
had called them on the ride back so they wouldn't worry about
finding his bed empty. Sherman declined Aubrey's offer to come in
for some ginger beer and, fighting a yawn, headed home.

Will brought Harley and Aubrey up to speed on the evening's
events, then took the two letters out from their plastic wrapping.
To gain time, they agreed to each read one and share the summary.
One letter was from Lily to Papineau, the other from Consul
Maxwell Allen to Lily. They decided to read them in the order in
which they had been written.

Lily's letter was first, as it was written on August 15, 1864,
which meant she hadn't yet received Papineau's letter to her — the
one Will had taken from Ord's office. In this letter, Lily worried

about the outbreak of yellow fever in St. George, and encouraged
Papineau to think about moving his base of operations to Halifax.

Lily said she knew that sailing from Halifax was longer and
meant carrying more coal for the extended round trip, meaning
that there would be less room for profitable cargo. But she stated
bluntly that if he died of yellow fever, he wouldn't be earning
anything. She also stressed that Halifax was one of the few ports
that could repair steel-hulled ships. There were a growing number
of blockade runners now operating in Halifax with sailors whose
drunkenness, loose morals, and arrogance, especially toward blacks,
were accepted by Haligonians as the price of renewed prosperity.

There was, of course, mention of being a more present father
to their son, who never stopped asking about him, asking when
he was coming home. She said the boy had held his *carte de visite*
so often that it had frayed. She also suggested that she felt they
would be financially stable if he simply sold his shares in the boat
and came home in one piece.

Apparently Major Walker, the Confederate agent in St. George,
had moved his family there to escape the epidemic of yellow
fever. On August 30, Alexander Keith Jr. had entertained him
and the creepy Dr. Luke Blackburn. She added, "That beastly
man, Alexander Keith Jr., has fronted marine insurance for
Southern owners, but when the boats sank, he collected the
insurance and never remitted a penny to the true owners." He
was making enemies and he knew it because Lily found a pistol
under his pillow.

The letter from US Consul Maxwell Allen was a very sad one.
He informed Lily with great regret that her husband, Papineau
Benoit, had succumbed to yellow fever two days after surviving
his own shipwreck. Allen went on to explain that he used all
the influence he could muster to have Papineau, the man who
had saved him from the penniless drunkard Villiers Rougemont,

buried in the north-west corner of St. Peter's graveyard. He told Lily it would be best if she came to Bermuda to settle the estate.

Will, Harley, and Aubrey stood looking around with a dejected air. They had come to like Papineau and his family. For a moment, Will felt like he was diving again, with everything floating in *Wavelength*'s cabin —nothing clear, with nothing moving forward with noticeable speed.

Then a thought struck him and he said, "Papineau didn't die of yellow fever. He couldn't have."

"What do you mean?" asked Harley.

"Right after his shipwreck, Papineau swam a mile to shore, rented a salvage boat, dove to recover his Whitworth cannons, hired a cart and driver and rode with him, passing Villiers Rougemont on the way," blurted Will. "It takes a few days for someone struck by yellow fever to die. They get progressively sicker and weaker before they die. He said it himself. He faked his illness on the boat, then did all those things only a strong man could do," said Will, nodding his head in support of his own theory.

"Why would Consul Allen say that if it wasn't true?" asked Harley.

Will shrugged. "I don't know, maybe he believed it. There was an epidemic of yellow fever in St. George in July of 1864, that's why that Major Walker took his family to Halifax, right?"

"What if he didn't die?" After allowing that statement to sink in, Harley explained, "What if he faked his death to make off with the money?"

"You mean cheat his wife out of the money?" asked Aubrey doubtfully.

"I don't know, but it is possible. He wouldn't be the first one to fake his death to make off with the family's wealth, right?" asked Harley in a tone that said even she wasn't totally convinced.

"If he faked it, how could his death certificate be registered in the Bermuda Archives in Hamilton?" asked Will. From his wallet he pulled out the note he'd scribbled in the archives when he'd followed Bennett inside. The entry for Papineau Benoit, aged thirty-nine, who had died on August 2, 1864, listed the cause of death as yellow fever. But what made Will's hair stand on end was the name of the witness, a name that hadn't rung a bell when he'd first read it: Dr. Luke Blackburn.

Will tapped the note and pointed to the first letter they'd just read. "Dr. Blackburn was in Halifax plotting with Alexander Keith Jr. on July 30. He couldn't have been seen in Halifax by Lily on July 30 and witnessed his death in Bermuda on August 2nd. No boat was that fast.

"So," said Aubrey, frowning, "somebody pretended to be Dr. Blackburn and declared Papineau died of yellow fever?"

"So who's buried in St. Peter's graveyard, if anybody?" asked Harley.

Less than an hour later, Aubrey parked his truck in St. George and he, Will, and Harley climbed the wall into St. Peter's cemetery. They made their way to the north-west corner and wove their way through the tombs to the one marked, "Papineau Benoit, born Bouctouche, New Brunswick, died St. George, August 2, 1864."

They looked at the tomb's beveled top, which as Aubrey explained, sat above ground on soil made up mostly of stone. Will and Harley looked around nervously. Aubrey squatted and looked at the underside before saying, "The mortar's quite gone and what's left is soft. Wouldn't take much to, you know, spring the lid free."

"You mean open the grave?" Apprehension crept into Harley's voice.

Aubrey dashed back to his truck and reappeared armed with a small crowbar. He ran the sharp tip along the inside where the mortar was supposed to seal the lid to the tomb. Will thought it made so much noise everybody in St. George could hear it. But if they did, they were either used to grave robbers or exceedingly tolerant of nocturnal noises, because nobody challenged them.

Aubrey signaled for Will and Harley to take the far end while he grappled with the other. He tapped the air with his index finger once, twice, and on the third stroke they heaved the lid to the side till it slid off, its edge resting on the tomb beside it.

Will and Harley jumped back as Aubrey shifted his weight backward. But he held the light steady and there was no doubt that there was a skeleton here, covered by wisps of cotton clothing that hadn't completely rotted away. Will held his breath as Harley did the same.

Harley pointed to the thighbone. It wasn't in a straight line like the other one. It had been staggered and had healed in a way that shortened the bone. That would explain why Papineau had limped. It was him — at least, likely him.

Will stared at the skull of the man he had known through his letters and his visions. He seemed like such a nice man. Will's eye caught something and he gestured to Aubrey for his flashlight.

When he moved the beam over the ribs, they saw two small bullets wedged into the back of a rib. Papineau hadn't died of yellow fever.

They looked at each other and nodded before shifting the cover back on and leaving the graveyard.

Nobody spoke till they'd jumped back into Aubrey's truck and locked the doors. Will said, "Those two bullets were really small caliber."

"And they were close together," said Harley. "Villiers Rouge-mont had a small bore, double-barreled derringer, remember? If I were betting on it …" she said, letting the thought go unfinished.

They didn't talk again till they drove across the bridge by the airport as the headlight caught the "walk your horse across" sign.

"So they killed him so Papineau wouldn't talk about the plot to ship clothes infected with yellow fever to the north," said Harley. "And the blood on his shirt from the two small bullets would have been mistaken for blood vomited by a victim of yellow fever and they would have been in a hurry to dispose of the infected body."

"Yellow fever doesn't spread by contact," said Aubrey. "It's a mosquito-borne disease."

"But they didn't know that back then, right?" asked Harley. "That's why the port of Charleston quarantined boats from Bermuda. That's why Dr. Blackburn thought shipping infected clothes to the north would spread the disease. So Villiers Rougemont didn't kill him for the coins because Consul Allen said he was a penniless drunk. He killed him to stop him from talking about their plot. Just like Claire Calloway killed Bennett to stop him from talking about Papineau's gold coins."

"Which she'll likely find if she finds Trotters' Trail before us," said Harley.

Aubrey turned to them and said, "I know where Trotters' Trail is located."

Chapter Twenty-four

Trotters' Trail

*Wainscoting: Wood paneling, usually from the ground up
to mid-wall or higher, often using thin strips of
tongue-and-groove pine or hard wood.*

As the sun crested over the horizon, Aubrey drove past a restaurant called Henry the VIII. "When I was a boy, the roof was covered in huge turtle shells and you could smell turtle soup cooking for miles around. Conservation practises put an end to that or we'd have wiped out the species by now."

They passed the Turtle Hill golf course, now empty in the early dawn. "Before that was a golf course, it was a pig farm. Papineau must 'a bought a piece of land from the farmer and built his cottage here."

"How'd you know it was called Trotters' Trail?" asked Harley.

"I worked with my father in the quarry. Must'a been six or seven when my dad was called to Trotters' Trail to fix the roof. Even back then people had stopped calling it that, but my dad remembered the old name." Aubrey pulled his truck up along the driveway entrance to a house. In the headlights and the faint morning light, they could see a big chain and padlock blocking their access. There was a for sale sign by the Ord Real Estate Company.

"Mr. Ord had a reputation as a slumlord," explained Aubrey. "He'd rent it for as long as he could, then sell it off."

They stepped out and peered over the "Private Property, No Trespassing" sign at a derelict one-story house with what appeared to be two chimneys.

They waited for a scooter to pass and looked around to be sure they weren't watched. They vaulted the sagging, rusty chain that blocked the driveway. The roof that Aubrey had worked on almost sixty years ago had two holes in it that showed wooden beams beneath that had grayed in the sun like the bones of an animal. Instead of it being a bright white roof like most Bermudian houses, this one was black with soot.

The doors and windows were locked. Aubrey pointed out the hatch to the cistern. A hundred or so years after Papineau had built Trotters' Trail, the owners had erected an addition. There were two cisterns; this one opened into a cupboard in the new kitchen, if one can call a sixty-year-old addition new.

Aubrey led them through it in a crouch. Because nobody had cleaned the gutters of leaves and other debris, water no longer gathered in the cistern. It was damp but without water.

The three intruders crawled out of the cupboard. They cautiously circled the living room where rain had warped the wide floorboards. Harley pointed to the fireplace, "I guess the mural that was painted there is long gone, huh? Who was that painter again?"

"Edward James," answered Will. Wainscoting encased the chimney above the mantle. Its once-white paint now peeled in long curls. Rot had eaten away at a couple of boards where they rested on the mantle and reached to the ceiling. A mouse had taken advantage of the soft wood to chew a hole.

Will borrowed Aubrey's flashlight, and pointed his beam through the hole. Seeing something, he crooked his index finger in the golf-ball-sized opening and tugged on it. A huge section of the wainscoting crashed to the living room floor.

"Wow," said Will.

"Holy wow," added Harley as she stepped up to where Will stood gawking.

The painting was in amazingly good shape. It was about six feet wide by four feet high. In the background, Trotters' Trail was caught in her prime, standing out beautifully in the blazing Bermudian sun. At the gate, smiling, were a man and a woman holding a baby. The man was Papineau Benoit, just like he looked in the photo on Papineau's *carte de visite*. He had the same dark hair, same square, squat features. Only Edward James had made him look happier in the painting than he did in the photo.

The three spread out to explore each room, each cupboard and pantry. They ran fingers along high ledges. In short, they did a thorough search of Trotters' Trail for a clue as to what had become of those double eagles that had not been found in the money box on the wreck. Coughs echoed through the house because their search raised only dust as their hopes sank.

Dejected, they clustered around the fireplace as if seeking warmth now that the trail had gone cold. Will looked to the fresco, then through the shore-side window to the gateposts by the ocean. He squinted because something was different. He walked over to the window and peered through the salt streaks to get a better look, compared what he saw to the fresco, and said, "It's not the same."

Harley and Aubrey shuffled over to him. "The wall in the fresco, painted while Papineau was alive, is a short wall, knee-high at best. The wall out there," he said, pointing outside, "built up after his death, is a lot higher. And there's something else that's different. Very different," teased Will, his mood brightening.

Harley snapped her fingers and said, "The gateposts. There

were no gateposts leading to the dock when it was painted." They hurried back out, through the cistern, up through the manhole, and down toward the ocean.

Aubrey squatted by the wall, drew a finger along the middle and said, "This is where the old wall stopped and you can see where it was built up later."

Will gave the rusty pintail a couple of whacks with a big stone, loosening the old mortar. The pintail, bits of stone, and mortar all fell away. Will pointed the flashlight beam into the crevice where the pintail had been. He jumped back onto the wall and, with the stone, banged the top of the gatepost off. He used the rusty pintail to scrape away the bits of mortar, slipped his hand into the opening, and felt around.

"These are the cannons. I can feel the rifling in them. I'm pretty sure these are the Whitworth cannons he salvaged," said Will with excitement.

"Then Lily was the one who buried them, maybe because the canons and the fresco were too painful a memory to keep around," mused Harley.

"And with the war at an end," said Aubrey, "not much demand for cannons in a market flooded with surplus ordnance. But we can't just take them. No matter what we think of Mr. Ord, they still belong to him or his estate."

The three of them looked back and forth between the two gateposts until a little smile crept onto Will's face and he waved Harley over and explained his plan.

Harley called the number on the real estate sign and asked for the property manager. That individual was only too willing to let Mr. Aubrey Dill, the stone-cutter and famous cricketer, repair the gateposts and take pictures to showcase his company. There was one stipulation. Aubrey had to take all the rubble away and not leave it on the property.

They rushed to the quarry, cut the necessary stone, but with the motorized saws for speed. They spent the afternoon removing the old stone and replacing it with new stone and fresh mortar. Time had not robbed Aubrey of either skill or speed. They were quick to cover the rusty cannons with a tarp after they'd been liberated from their stone tombs. With everything shipshape and new galvanized pintails embedded and waiting for an eventual gate, Aubrey had wheelbarrowed the small scraps into the back of the truck.

The breeches on the cannons had long rusted shut. But the openings had merely been covered over by the thin layer of Bermuda stone that Will had knocked loose. Using the jack from the truck they raised the breech, which lowered the mouth of the cannon — nothing came out. Will rammed a long branch into it. Bits of rotten cloth came out. When they jacked the breech higher a bucketful of coins flooded out in front of them. The second cannon yielded up at least as many double eagle coins. They'd found Papineau's fortune through the mouth of his cannons.

Chapter Twenty-five

Amazing Grace

*"Amazing Grace": A widely sung Christian hymn that speaks
of redemption, composed by Pastor John Newton. Although it
was later sung as a hymn against slavery, Newton did not
compose it for that reason because it was only years after
composing it that he opposed slavery.*

Will, Harley and Aubrey each picked up a coin, studied them, and
let out a collective whoop. They had found Papineau Benoit's
double eagles.

Will suddenly had the feeling they were being watched. He
scanned the trees on either side of the property and walked up
a bit till he could see the road — nothing. He urged Harley and
Aubrey to get the coins off the property.

Aubrey said he couldn't haul the cannons up to the truck
without destroying either his truck or the property and likely
both. So they thought about that a moment till Harley blurted,
"Sherman. Let's ask him if he can come and get us by boat.
You can come back for the truck later, Aubrey."

Sherman said he'd be there in thirty minutes. They rolled the
cannons down to the wharf and onto a sectional floating dock
that just managed to stay above water.

When Sherman saw all the gold coins his knees buckled and he slumped to the gunwale, took off his baseball cap and fanned himself with it despite the strong offshore breeze. "I have never seen such wealth in one spot at one time, no sir, no sir."

They put the coins into one of Sherman's empty fish coolers. He threw his arms out in puzzlement.

Harley explained how Bennett had found letters from his ancestor that spoke of the blockade runner *Lily* that had sunk opposite the boilers while laden with gold. He had brought the Edward James' painting of *Lily* to sell to Brian Ord with the hopes of financing an illegal salvage operation.

Will jumped in and explained how Ord, who owned the painting's twin by Edward James offered to become partners in the illegal wreck dive. But when he got cold feet, Claire Calloway let Ord die and dressed like him to create the impression that Ord was still alive. She was the one who had locked Bennett in *Wavelength*'s cabin and blew it up.

Towing the floating dock wouldn't allow them to gain speed but they'd be at Aubrey's place in about an hour. They had moved offshore maybe a mile when a Boston Whaler suddenly roared right up to them.

The man behind the hat and sunglasses was Drury. Claire Calloway sat beside him with her pistol pointed at them, saying, "I think you have something that belongs to me."

Claire stepped into the stern of Sherman's boat. With one hand she tied her boat to Sherman's. Drury tied a bow line onto Sherman's, then joined Calloway.

"You probably thought we'd left the island," she said with a faint smile. "Problem is, it takes money to travel. And when you," she said looking at Will, "exposed me to the police, well they put a freeze on Mr. Ord's bank accounts. I was counting on all those double eagles as my travelling money but we weren't as lucky as you. So now, I'll take what's rightfully mine," she said, sitting on the transom and resting her gun on her lap but in a manner that said she could shoot before anybody took a step forward.

"This isn't your money," said Aubrey. "You didn't find it, these two did," he said waving a finger between Will and Harley.

"Who do you think identified that Edward James painting as authentic? I knew we were onto something good and if that idiot Ord hadn't lost his nerve, we would have taken our time and found those double eagles. So where are they?" she asked, raising her gun.

When the silence grew too long, she said, "Look, I can shoot you one at a time or you can show me now and we leave you to float for a few hours."

Aubrey flipped the fish cooler open and pointed at its contents. Claire got up and smiled when she ran her free hand through the mound of gold coins. "I'm going to assume it's all there. Well, it's been fun, but I have to say goodbye. Which of you two bothersome brats is first?" She swiveled her gun from Will to Harley.

Aubrey stepped in front of them and swept them behind him with his long arms. "You won't be hurting my friends."

"Well, isn't that chivalrous. Okay, you first." She leveled the gun at Aubrey's chest.

"Wait a minute Claire," said Drury sidling up to her. "You said we were just going to take the coins and disable their motor and radio."

"Oh, Drury, wake up. We'll need a few hours to get a sailboat and make our way to Florida. Somebody will see them long before that and we'll be lucky to leave Bermuda's territorial waters." Calloway raised her gun in a two-handed grip.

"That's Aubrey Dill. You can't kill Bermuda's most famous cricketer. You can't," blurted Drury.

"You either kill or be killed," she said without taking her eyes off Aubrey.

Drury sprang, wrestling with her till the gun went off. Aubrey was struck by the bullet and spun around, blood flying from his head as he spiraled onto the gunwale, toppling overboard.

"Aubrey!" yelled Will.

Drury was in a death grip with Calloway. The gun went off two more times and they pitched off the stern.

With a life ring in hand, Will leaped overboard, splashing into the filament of blood trailing after Aubrey's inert form. Will kicked his way forward and grabbed him with one arm. As he turned back to the boat, Sherman scrambled down the flying deck. He and Harley pulled Aubrey and Will aboard.

Sherman whipped open his first-aid kit and put a compress against Aubrey's bleeding scalp. There was no sign of either Calloway or Drury.

They tied the floating dock with the cannons to the boat Calloway had used and dropped its anchor so it wouldn't drift and damage coral or another boat. After alerting the Bermuda police, Sherman raced all the way to the hospital.

A few hours later Will, Harley, and Sherman paced in the waiting room at the King Edward VII Memorial Hospital. After being treated in the Emergency Ward, Aubrey had been wheeled into a private room, still unconscious. The doctors had said that time would tell how he would do. The sooner he responded to outside stimulus, the likelier he was to recover. They were not prepared to let them in because they weren't family.

Will finally sat looking at his hands, Harley beside him. Sherman huddled with a handful of members of the church choir, whispering and nodding to encourage each other that the outcome would be positive.

The doors flew open and Hamlet padded his way across the tiled floor with Dr. Doan holding a leash that had no slack.

The duty nurse jumped up, "Sorry, Dr. Doan, there are no

dogs allowed —"

Dr. Doan and Hamlet were already through the next set of doors as she called back, "What dog?" She cupped her left hand for Will and Harley to follow. Sherman and the choir didn't wait to ask if they were included, they just came.

Will skipped ahead to Aubrey's room. He leaned over and whispered, "You can go back in the water if you need to, Aubrey. I just want you to know that as your friend, whatever you choose, I'll understand and I'll be on shore waiting."

"Give us a sign," whispered Dr. Doan to Aubrey, who lay with his eyes closed, his head wrapped in a thin gauze turban. Hamlet jumped up at the end of the bed, his tail tap, tap, tapping gently, staring at Aubrey's ashen face as if he understood the gravity of the situation. Sherman and the choir shuffled in, forming a horseshoe-shaped support group at the foot of his bed.

The only sounds came from pinched nostrils and machines that beeped the status quo. Will took one of Aubrey's hands into his and Dr. Doan took the other.

Without knowing why, Will started to sing "Amazing Grace." But his voice broke as he sang, "how sweet the sound."

Without missing a beat, Sherman and the choir stepped in, their voices clear and strong. Then he felt it. Aubrey's hand twitched. Will and Dr. Doan looked across at each other because she'd felt it too — and so had the machines, which beeped.

A doctor rushed in with two nurses in her wake. Without being asked, everyone, Hamlet included, made their way back to the waiting room.

Sherman came up behind Will and slipped a big hand on his shoulder. "Well done, Will. Hey, you should be happy, he, he, Aubrey responded. He's going to make it. Sure as fish swim."

Will looked up, "Darwin said it isn't the strong or the clever who survive, it is those who can adapt. After all he's been through, do you think he can adapt and survive?"

Sherman looked back toward Aubrey's room. "If I can adapt and change, so can Aubrey Dill."

Will gave Sherman a puzzled look, so the fisherman explained, "You remember me telling you about how I became a member of Aubrey's congregation and eventually a friend after the men from my parish pushed over his walls?"

Will nodded.

"Well, I was one of those men who pushed over the walls to his house on that first night." He paused to let the weight of that information sink in. "If a dark, hateful soul like mine can adapt and grow toward the light, the generous soul of Aubrey Dill will not fail to do the same. No sir, no sir."

Historical Notes

There are a number of historical characters in this novel. Joseph Hayne Rainey was a free black man who escaped to Bermuda with his wife and who operated a lucrative barbershop in the basement of Tucker House in St. George where he taught himself to read and write. His wife ran a successful dress shop in Hamilton. After the Civil War, he returned to the Carolinas and became the first black man elected to the US House of Representatives.

Edward James was a Brit who painted in Bermuda and he did sell his paintings to Consul Allen as well as a copy of the same boat to the blockade-running captains. Southern sailors who cut down his flagpole assaulted Consul Allen in St. George. Dr. Luke Blackburn was arrested in Montreal and charged with violating Canada's neutrality laws for trying to transport through Canada trunks full of clothes that had belonged to people who died of yellow fever in Bermuda. But when the judge asked to see the trunks with the clothes, prosecutors admitted that they'd burnt them to avoid contagion. The judge told them they'd burnt their evidence and he had no choice but to release Blackburn who would eventually be elected Governor of Kentucky.

The Bermuda Archives did not start recording deaths till after the Civil War so I have taken creative license.

Books: *The Dynamite Fiend* by Ann Larabee offers an in-depth look at the disturbing life of Alexander Keith Jr., the Nova Scotia brewmaster's nephew, swindler, Confederate spy, and homicidal psychopath. For good measure, Ms. Larabee brings to life Dr. Luke Blackburn's links to Keith and his attempts at biological warfare. Bruce Catton's *Terrible Swift Sword* is often considered the definitive book on the Civil War. I have consulted a number of other books including: *Dispatches from Bermuda* (Consul Allen's dispatches), edited by Glen N. Wiche; *Rogues & Runners, Bermuda and the American Civil War*, published by the Bermuda National Trust; Stephen R. Wise's *Lifeline of the Confederacy, Blockade Running During the Civil War, From Cape Charles to Cape Fear; The North Atlantic Blockading Squadron during the Civil War* by Robert M. Browning Jr.; and *Tallahassee Skipper* by Arthur Thurston.

While I do my best to refurbish history with accuracy, I accept that any errors in this endeavor are mine alone.

Acknowledgements

As usual, my early readers include Clarinda, Liliana, Julien, Rich, Erica, and Dom Fiore. Without Liliana and Rich's frequent hospitality in Bermuda I could not have written this book. Jack Grin, Marianne Fedunkiw, and Ernie Boulton brought constructive criticism to bear on the story. Marian Hebb keeps me on the straight and legal. Barbara Fullerton was the first to inform me of Bermuda's colorful past. Dusty Hind helped bring Bermuda's artistic history into focus, while Dr. Edward Harris and Elena Strong shared their knowledge of the island's nautical past. Charles Gossling took time from his busy life to share his understanding of Bermuda life, Lance Furbert told me how he brought Joseph Rainey to life during his many historical reenactments, Chris Gauntlet, who operates Blue Water Divers, took me diving on the Civil War blockade runner the *Marie Celeste* and over the course of a number of meetings and a ride on his fishing boat, fisherman Michael Barnes helped me flesh out the character of Aubrey's best friend Sherman. The good people at Windridge Farms allowed me to observe their therapeutic work from up close.

Friend and gifted golfer Phillip James and his uncle Lloyd James defined the demanding world of the Bermuda stonecutter. Former Bermuda Police Commissioner and former Chief Superintendent of the RCMP, Jean-Jacques Lemay, kindly introduced me to the Bermuda Police. Sergeant Paul Watson patiently explained the many responsibilities of the Bermuda police's marine unit and their attendant protocols. P.C. Colin Mill took me for a four-hour ride along in one of the police boats and took me over to meet famed diver and treasure hunter Teddy Tucker. Real estate agent Donna Bennett drove me around till we found a stand-in for my fictitious cottage called Trotters' Trail. The Honorable David Saul made time for coffee at the Rock Island Coffee Shop and a long chat about treasure hunting. Professor Michael Jarvis, along with Katie Law and the staff at the Rogues & Runners Museum in St. George, were generous in sharing their knowledge of Bermuda's past.

The characters in this book are fictitious and are made up of various bits and pieces I heard about different people, and all alloyed to my imagination.

This novel is dedicated to the memory of

Joseph Hayne Rainey

*A free black man, he fled the Carolinas at the outbreak of
the American Civil War and
became a prosperous barber in St. George, Bermuda.
During his exile, he taught himself what was illegal
for a black man in the South: to read and write.
After the war, he returned to the Carolinas and became
the first black man elected to the US House of Representatives.*